BARBARA YATES
ROTHWELL

AN EMPTY BOTTLE

AND OTHER TALES

Order this book online at www.trafford.com
or email orders@trafford.com

Most Trafford titles are also available at major online book retailers.

Printed in the United States of America.

ISBN: 978-1-4669-6110-4 (hc)
ISBN: 978-1-4669-6108-1 (sc)
ISBN: 978-1-4669-6109-8 (e)

Library of Congress Control Number: 2012918427

Trafford rev. 10/12/2012

www.trafford.com

North America & international
toll-free: 1 888 232 4444 (USA & Canada)
phone: 250 383 6864 ♦ fax: 812 355 4082

FOR MY LOVELY FAMILY

WHICH IS NOW MORE LIKE A CLAN

About the Author

BARBARA YATES ROTHWELL lived, married and brought up six children in Surrey, England, before immigrating to Western Australia in 1974 with her musician husband and their two youngest daughters. Her other children arrived in Australia in due course. Also a musician and a trained singer, she was for ten years in the 1980s a music reviewer for *The West Australian newspaper.*

After founding and running the Yanchep Community School for eight years, and having successfully written and sold innumerable short stories and articles to major magazines in several countries, Barbara decided it was time to branch out into novel writing. Longman Cheshire published her teenage historical novel, THE BOY FROM THE HULKS, in 1994 (now reprinted), and in 1998 her historical novel DUTCH POINT was published privately in England.

In 2004 she joined forces with Trafford Publishing (Canada) to produce COULTER VALLEY, an Australian story tracing the effects on a family of artists of a despotic father; and in 2005 the same cooperation produced KLARA, fiction based on fact, the story of a German Jewess who, forced to leave Nazi Germany, was sponsored by an English family. RIPPLE IN THE REEDS (2006) tells the story of a French girl, who marries against her parents' wishes and finds herself in wartime Germany. A new life awaits her in Australia—until the past catches up.

In 2007 Barbara collected 20 of her short stories under the title of NO TIME FOR PITY and Other Tales. This was followed by two more collections: STANDFAST and AN EMPTY BOTTLE.

Barbara was a journalist in the UK for several years, as Women's Page Editor for a large group of weekly papers in the south of England, and as a free-lance. She has also written two full-length and several one-act plays, which have been performed in community theatres in Western Australia and New South Wales.

Some comments . . .

. . . on books by Barbara Yates Rothwell

Dutch Point (1998: The Lagoon Press)

' . . . DUTCH POINT runs to 471 pages and every word is worth reading. A thoroughly enjoyable and thought-provoking tale.' M.B.

' . . . successfully transports the reader back in time to the dubious beginnings of the Australian colonies . . . ' The Wanneroo Times.

' . . . what a wonderful book it is. I couldn't put it down—so if they complain I'm sleepy at work it is your fault.' C.F.

Coulter Valley (2004: Trafford Publishing in cooperation with The Lagoon Press)

'What a fine book! . . . a great achievement . . . the novel amounts to a huge paradox: a celebration of art . . . the necessity of devoting oneself to art's disciplines, and . . . a red light against obsession and oppression.' D.C.

' . . . a viable alternative for readers weary of the latest inanc blockbuster . . . Barbara Yates Rothwell has something interesting to say.' The West Australian.

Klara (2005: Trafford Publishing in cooperation with The Lagoon Press)

'A truly magnificent read and not one to be missed. Klara is fiction, but based on fact.' Sun City News.

'Klara is a well researched, fascinating read.' North Coast Times.

Ripple in the Reeds (2006: Trafford Publishing): A French girl marries a young Nazi before WWII and lives to regret it.

The Boy from the Hulks (1994: Longman Cheshire, Melbourne) now in second edition with Trafford: ' . . . a quality yarn ideally suited for the English and history curricula of junior secondary schools . . . potentially a very big market.' The West Australian.

'Author spins a bonzer yarn.' The Wanneroo Times.

Three collections of short stories: _No Time for Pity_; _Standfast_; _The Empty Bottle_.

Softback: $25.00 each.

Dutch Point is available from www.barbarayatesrothwell.com
hardback: $30.00

Coulter Valley, Klara and *Ripple in the Reeds* can be ordered
from *Trafford.com* and the author. $30.00

*Barbara Yates Rothwell, 6 Nautical Court, Yanchep, W. Australia
6035. Phone: 61 8 9561 1125
Email: morgand_h.byr@iinet.net.au
Trafford Publishing, 1663 Liberty Drive, Suite 200, Bloomington
IN 47403, USA. www.Trafford.com*

Front cover watercolour by the author, May 2010.

THE LONG AND THE SHORT OF IT

I t is generally believed (by publishers, chiefly) that short story collections are no longer popular with readers. Having conducted my own (admittedly small) survey, among young mums, hard-working businesswomen and senior citizens, I am encouraged to think that the short story genre is not yet dead. When leisure time is brief, or when something less demanding than a novel is wanted just before sleep, what could be better than a good short story?

What, though, is the real difference between novels and short stories—apart from length, of course? Is a short story simply a cut-down novel? Is a novel simply a long short story? Well—no.

The two genres are separate and different in a number of ways. Novelists are not necessarily good short story creators, and vice versa, though many are. It is much the same in music. Writers of symphonic works are also not necessarily composers of small-scale chamber music—but many of them do it supremely well.

A good short story will have no loose ends, no meanderings through the plot, no unnecessary characters, and limited but effective descriptions. The plot may well be comparatively simple—but it's a good idea to have a twist in the tail.

The main characters will go through a process which will in some way change them, possibly resolve a problem, perhaps clear up a past mystery. The stories can be complex but the writing must be pared down. Non-essential words have to go.

It is common, when writing a short story, to realise that there are too many characters, and then one must cut. No matter that Jasper is one of the best characters you have ever created—if he has no real reason for being there, he must go. Use him somewhere else.

Novels present the opposite problem. It is not unusual to discover that, if the book is not to become a major bore, new characters will have to be introduced, perhaps halfway through.

This is where the sub-plot comes in. And it works, as long as the sub-plot has relevance to the major story.

How long should a short story be? This is first cousin to 'how long is a piece of string?' Because these stories are often written for commercial magazines they will seldom be longer than 2500 words. So-called 'literary magazines' will take something longer. But the rules still apply. Whatever the style of writing, there will be no room in the well-written story for any padding. And for the dedicated short story writer, finding a way to involve the reader without metres of description is a big part of the attraction. Atmosphere is one way of doing this. Deciding on characters and venue is essential, but if the writing conveys atmosphere as well it is probably an effectively created piece of work.

Commercialism—that is, writing for the magazines—need not mean selling one's soul, though the knowledge that one occasionally 'writes for the mags' does sometimes create an atmosphere of its own. One well-known author attacked me quite rudely on the subject. How could I write for money? (I presume she meant, how could I so demean a sacred gift?). Easily, I said. I have a large family. Besides, while there are practitioners in all branches of the arts who can justly be called 'artists', there are many more who are happy to be described as craftsmen and women. And there are many—of whom my sarcastic friend was one—who accept very large grants to support their writing passion. How is this more desirable than earning it?

May I hope that among the stories I have collected in these pages you will find a few that please? I am open to comment on contact@barbarayatesrothwell.com

Index

AN EMPTY BOTTLE

I had a wonderful holiday recently, during which I crossed Canada, having first visited friends in San Francisco: my first trip to the American continent. In San Francisco my host, knowing that in my youth, long years ago, I had been temporarily destined for an artistic career, took me to his watercolour class one evening.

I was afraid I would make a complete fool of myself. We were, after all, talking about something back where dinosaurs roamed. I hadn't painted anything except a few doors and window frames since school. But I gave in under pressure, determining that if I was to be proved a sham I would do it with style.

I took with me an empty wine bottle. Making glass look like glass with paint on paper is not easy. I was in a challenging mode. I set up my 'model', adjusted some lighting, and began to splash the paint on. And I got quite carried away. Perhaps, I was thinking, I should after all have followed my artistic star! And I found I not only enjoyed what I was doing, but that others were quite interested in what I had achieved. That was a notable evening.

Someone said, 'You should use it as a cover for your next book'. But to do that (the next book was to be a collection of short stories) I would have to have a story to go with it.

And this is it!

AN EMPTY BOTTLE

When the south-westerly blows, the sea is stirred with excitement and the white tops wear their caps rakishly. On the beach, people relax instinctively after a week of summer heat. Autumn is welcome.

We've been coming here, Janice and I, for the past three years, since that amazing day when she walked into my life. Almost exactly three years, as it happens, since Dave said, 'James, I don't believe you've met Janice'. She walked into my life—and now she has walked out of it.

We come to this little restaurant with its panoramic view of the Indian Ocean—I suppose I should say *we used to come*, because Janice was, in her usual direct way, quite calmly determined.

'Yes, I know, James—it's been good. But good things come to an end, don't they?'

I think I said, 'why?' If it's good, why stop? I'd expected permanency. I hadn't imagined that I was a temporary filling for a gap in her life. She didn't answer my question—my stupefied question. Honestly, I hadn't expected this.

Between us, the table held the debris of our meal—plates, wineglasses, cutlery, an empty wine bottle. A waiter appeared as I was struggling for something to say that wouldn't lower me in my own estimation. I would have liked to roar my pain. But I don't think Janice does pain.

The table debris disappeared, balanced precariously, leaving only the wine bottle. Stupidly, because I didn't know what to say at a time like this, I nodded towards it. 'Would you like another?'

She was getting ready to go, and shook her head. 'Better if I just leave.' She regarded me thoughtfully for a moment. 'Look after yourself, James. You're quite a special person, you know.'

'But not quite special enough.' Briefly she shook her head and was gone. She was gone, and I hadn't even stretched out a hand to stop her. I saw her through the window, getting into her car, reversing out, turning and leaving. No one could tell, I was thinking, that anything, *anything* had just taken place, here in this little restaurant that we had both enjoyed. I wondered what I could have done to prevent it. Was it my fault? Am I so boring? She had never given me any idea that she found me so. I didn't think we were incompatible, but how can you tell? Even with someone you thought you were really close to, understood thoroughly, loved to distraction—how can you tell what *the other* is thinking?

I've been sitting here for a long time, alone in my misery. When I suddenly found myself, came to myself, I suppose, the sun had moved around; the water is now sparkling like diamonds. I stare at that for a while, thinking that perhaps if I had insisted on an engagement, bought diamonds for her instead of relying on the sun and the sea to do it for me, today might never have happened. But I knew, somewhere deep, that it wouldn't have worked. My life view of walking together in sunlight, perhaps each holding a pair of small hands, running on the beach with dogs, was just a mirage. Now that I had been shown reality I could see that Janice would never have been the maternal woman that I had shaped her into in my thoughts.

There's a not quite hot cup of coffee on the table. Did I order it? I don't remember doing so. I drink it and feel a shiver of life entering me. Somehow, I begin to realise, I have to get through the rest of the day, the rest of the week—the rest of my life? I have never felt so absolutely lonely.

It doesn't help that there are three couples in the restaurant, mocking my isolation. The nearest ones are young, ardent, smiling secretly, looking a bit coy. I resent their ability to gaze into each other's eyes. I have never realised how important it is to

2

have someone to look at so intimately, not needing to turn away, as one would with a friend. Of course—they're honeymooners! Half their luck! I feel mildly bitter for no good reason. All at once, at a signal I don't see, they stand and leave, his arm around her shoulders. Easy enough to guess how *they'll* spend the evening.

A couple of tables further on there are two much longer-married people. You can tell by the way *they* never gaze deeply into each other's eyes. Besides, there is the fruit of their love, a small boy with neat hair, sitting upright and not speaking. There is an indefinable air of ho-humness about the three of them. A 'been there, done that'. I wonder why they are here, on this particular day. I suppose they could be on holiday, but they are not wearing holiday clothes. They are as neat as the boy's hair, nothing out of place. Now and again one of them will speak. One will answer. Then more silence. I find myself fascinated by their lack of verve. I *will* them to speak to the child, or for him to speak to them.

Suddenly he does. His clear voice comes across to me. 'Can I go down to the beach, Mummy?'

'You'd better ask your father. This was his idea.'

Oh-oh! A clue. A rift in the happy family. What did Mama want to do today? The washing? Catch up with the carpet beating? Iron out of the bed linen any impulse to crease? I almost wish one of them would stand and shout, bang the table, anything but this deadening silence.

'Daddy?'

'Yes, son. Off you go.'

'But don't get dirty and wet.' That's Mama. The boy goes and I see him walking ever so carefully down to the sand, where he will undoubtedly get his polished shoes damp.

Father looks at Mother, a straight look into her eyes. But it's not like the honeymooners' gaze. 'It's not his fault,' he says in a low voice. 'Don't take it out on the kid.'

'I wish you wouldn't call him a kid,' she says. 'He's a boy.'

The man sighs. 'Oh, Marian,' he says and shakes his head. They gather their gear together and stand up. They walk out without touching. He turns to make sure they haven't left anything

3

behind. Is that what marriage becomes? I wonder. Would Janice and I have come to that silent, punishing place? Surely not! Yet we hadn't even made it to marriage, and nowhere near to parenthood. So how would I know?

In the far corner, by a window with a view of sea and sand, and dunes covered with foliage, sit an elderly couple. They have to be in their eighties. They don't gaze into each other's eyes, either, nor do they speak much. But there is such warmth coming from their little corner. They are holding hands on the table top, and now and then she pats his hand as if to reassure him that she is still there.

She pours out more tea for him and he drinks it noisily. She offers him a plate with two biscuits on it and he carefully chooses one—the chocolate one! I notice the hearing aid in the ear facing me; and when he turns his head I see there is a matching one on the other side. That explains the lack of talking, perhaps.

I wonder for a moment how long they have been married. Is this a celebration for sixty glorious years? Or did they meet in the retirement village and decide that two could live even more cheaply than one? Short of asking them I shall never know. But somehow there is something about them that gently lifts my spirits. I am thankful that it *is* possible to feel comfortable with another person; that some people, at least, are not alone on life's journey.

And that is when I all at once realise that I have never felt quite comfortable with Janice. I look back and see that I always had the sensation that I had to try, to work at it, to meet some standard which was never quite explained to me. I loved her, yes (already she is in the past tense, you see), but now I can see that I was on trial, and today was the verdict.

I notice, as I had not before in my dark mood, that she has left her glasses and diary on the table, partly hidden by the empty bottle, which for some reason has not been cleared away. I am glad; I shall take it home with me as a memento of a turning point in my life.

When she rings, perhaps this evening, and says in her imperious way, 'James, I think I left my sunnies and diary on the table. Could you send them on to me, please?' I shall say, 'No, Janice—you didn't leave anything behind'. And I shall look at the world, just once, through her glasses to see what she saw; but I shall not read the diary. I'll burn it. Burning is clean.

IN A SUMMER'S AFTERNOON

I really like some of those small, isolated Australian towns that have somehow managed to get themselves settled away from the cities and retained their individuality. I can imagine that if you were born and brought up in one of them, the memory and the feeling would remain with you even as you welcomed the additional comforts that cities offer.

I have a particular one in mind. I've called it Burton's Mill for the purposes of this tale. The child in all of us tends to reappear when we revisit the scenes of childhood—and sometimes the knowledge is enough to keep us away from that early home. But Fate has its way of leading us on into something we had not wanted. This happened to James.

IN A SUMMER'S AFTERNOON

I t is quite possible to avoid Burton's Mill. Most people do. By keeping straight on over the cross-roads and holding to the main highway one may arrive, in under three hours, at the city suburbs. This was what James had intended to do. Nostalgia could wait.

The car thought otherwise. One might expect a BMW of recent vintage with all the trimmings to be capable of a five-hour drive without difficulty; usually this was the case. But as the cross-roads came into view the car spluttered—quite genteel—coughed once or twice and made itself clear to its driver: *Have me looked at now. Later may be too late.*

So, unprepared for a trip into his past, James entered the main street of Burton's Mill; not with quite the sophisticated air he would have wished (the car had added hiccups to its other symptoms), but at least with a very good excuse, had he wanted one, for being there.

The mechanic wiped his fingers on an oily rag, pointed to obscure places in the car's innards and made a diagnosis. James, thankful that it was nothing too serious, had time to kill. He stood outside the garage and looked up and down the street, that typical dusty, somnolent main street of any small Australian country town; and was suddenly, not knowing why, unreasonably apprehensive.

He began to walk in the late summer sunshine, aimlessly at first; white-painted rails proclaimed a bridge ahead, surely the one over the creek, never quite dry even in summer, where long ago he had come to play.

A slow, steady flow was emerging from a culvert beneath the road. Somewhere, he recalled, there was a spring. Hadn't he and—what was the boy's name? Stan, Stephen?—hadn't they explored together, up among the thick undergrowth on the other side of the road, to find the source? He grinned slightly. Steve! He hadn't thought of him in—how long? Thirty years since . . . well, since James and his father had left the town. Thirty years! The grin faded. Steve had been less than a memory for three decades; yet once, as six-year-olds, they had lived in each other's pockets. Where was he now, little Steve with his home-made haircut, his patches and mended clothes?

James turned his back on the creek. The trees hanging over it and the densely growing ferns threatening to choke it made it dark, almost dank, and he shivered suddenly and moved on along the street.

Everyone says it—*never go back!* Just as they say that the revisited scenes of childhood always seem to have shrunk. True enough; James looked around him. This street, for instance; once it had seemed a long prospect, with excitement waiting behind certain windows: lollies at the place over the road, ice-creams from Mrs—Mrs . . . ? He snapped his fingers impatiently: Mrs March! An old woman, she was, with bad teeth and a permanent dislike of children. He wondered why she had bothered to sell a commodity guaranteed to attract them.

There used to be a café, he remembered, and then he saw it, half the size he had expected, in need of paint, its windows covered by drab net curtains. 'Green Parrot Tea Rooms'. The name rang no bells. What had it been in that other existence? Just *the café*; sometimes *Miss Petrie's place*, as in 'I'll meet you at Miss Petrie's place'. Who had said that? His mother? Surely not Father? It wasn't the sort of place fathers went to. Father went to the hotel for his evenings out. It had sometimes, he thought, been a bone of contention. His mother—all at once he saw her in a flash of memory! Standing by the sink in the dark, airless kitchen, her face white with anger and despair. He couldn't see Father. But where was he, himself, the six-year-old James? Standing behind

8

the door? Watching her as tears ravaged her face, frightened to stay there, frightened to go to bed—frightened?

He shivered again. Was this why he had never returned to Burton's Mill? Too many ghosts; too many inexplicable strands to be unravelled. Yet he had existed quite successfully in those years after, when he and Father had lived together in a variety of homes after Mother's death. If there had been stresses, they had not haunted him. Every small boy who loses his mother will have to come to terms with the fact. That's what he had told himself when, as the years passed, he occasionally sensed within himself a pang of loss, of deprivation, sometimes of incomprehensible fear.

He had loved his father—well, respected him. Even felt a mild affection at times. It was difficult to show love for a man so remote, so undemonstrative. But they had managed comfortably enough together until James went to university; then his father had said, 'I've done my best for you, son. Now it's up to you!' And he had gone: Europe first, then America, and then back to Europe where he died in a French train crash. James had not been devastated, but he had known a sense of abandonment, as if life itself had set him up to be solitary.

The Green Parrot was almost empty. A middle-aged woman came to him, pad and pencil at the ready. 'Just a pot of tea,' he said. Then 'Raisin toast!' surprising himself.

'Tea. Raisin toast', the woman repeated, and went away. Raisin toast? He never ate raisin toast. What fold of memory had thrown up that childhood treat? They would sit here, in the window where now he had automatically set himself, and Mother would say in her poshest voice, 'A pot of tea and some raisin toast'.

It had to have raisins. You poked them out, laughing up at Mum who was pretending to be shocked, and ate them, warm and squashy, off the end of your finger.

You would never do that with Father, even if he had taken you out to tea, which was inconceivable. You would sit up straight with Father, while he ate or drank or stared about him in an arrogant manner which was the chief thing you would remember once he had taken himself out of your life. You would have to grow

9

up before you were able to consider that perhaps the arrogance covered some failure of confidence.

'Passing through?' asked the woman as she placed tea and toast before him.

'In a way. My car broke down.' He hesitated, then: 'As a matter of fact I used to live here.'

'When was that?'

'When I was a child. We left after my mother died.'

'In the town, were you? Or out in the sticks?'

He wished he had kept the past to himself. 'In a cottage at the far end of town. I don't know if I'd recognise it again. I was very young.'

'Sentimental journey, then.' She nodded and went back behind the counter. James drank tea. One man's tragedy is another's passing incident. You can't bleed for the world.

With the taste of raisin bread still on his tongue James walked slowly along the hot, dusty road, past shops in need of paint, mothers with infants in pushers, old men staring across the street at nothing. It was familiar and yet strange to him. He felt he might recognise things better if he could crouch to a six-years-old's eye level, but he had no wish to draw attention to himself.

A narrow cross-road marked the end of the shopping street. He stood on the edge of the pavement; to the left, he suddenly recalled, was the paddock where he and Steve had played together and chased the cows. He corrected himself. That was where the paddock *had* been; it had been turned into an oval just before . . .

What had been to the right? He looked along to where the road curved out of sight. The school surely, the brick and weatherboard building where Miss—Miss . . . He saw Steve, hand up, frantically waving. 'Miss! Miss! Miss!'

'Miss *what?*' from a figure dimly seen in memory, a tall figure, unsmiling, yet a source of security.

'Miss Cooper, Miss.'

Miss Cooper. There had been something—Mother, was it, or Father? Someone had gone to school, taken him home, there had been a fuss. Afterwards Miss Cooper had said, 'You mustn't worry,

10

James. It's not your fault.' But he *had* worried, and somehow it *had* seemed to be his fault.

He'd walk along there later if he had the time. Perhaps.

Beyond the town centre the road grew narrow and leafy with eucalypts and acacias and the graceful drooping branches of peppermints. Sunbeams through dappled leaves brought him back to childhood, when he and Steve would climb high into the heart of a tree and sit there in the magic of green sunlight to read their comics.

He was unprepared for the cottage. It had seemed to young legs much further down the lane. It was small, so much smaller; paintwork was peeling faded green where once it had peeled weathered brown. James stood at the gate and stared. Small windows on either side of a ramshackle front door; a rusty tin roof with half a chimney; a lean-to with louvred windows—the laundry? At one side a ragged shrubbery, choking on its own untidiness; on the other a few square metres of scratched earth with a draggle of seedy vegetables.

A small, grubby dog rushed towards the gate, yapping furiously. From behind the cottage a young woman emerged; it was life repeating itself. The tired eyes, the slightly nervous manner. Perhaps the house had that effect on its occupants. 'Come here, Rocky!' She glanced up. 'She won't hurt you.' She came forward, bent to the dog's collar. 'You looking for something?'

He shook his head. 'I used to live here.'

'Well, lucky you!' She regarded him drily, wearily. 'You look as if you got out in time.'

'I was a little boy.'

She hesitated. 'Want to look round?'

He wanted to say no—but he said, 'Yes, if it's not inconvenient.'

She almost smiled. 'No, it's not inconvenient. Just unexpected.' She opened the gate, and the dog, reassured, assaulted his legs with desperate affection.

Time had stood still. He thought, *this has been a refuge for no-hopers. No one has imprinted it with character, with personal taste.* He stared around the tiny living room, through a half open door to the laundry piled with washing that would never have that TV-radiance about it, through another to a bedroom stark in its poverty. He turned; the woman was watching him with a self-mocking smile which said everything: *you in your expensive clothes, gold watch, gold and diamond signet ring—I in my dreariness—we have this bond, this common thread: we have lived in this dilapidation. Somewhere, somehow, we are buddies.*

'It seems smaller,' he said.

'It is small.' She leaned back against the door, her eyes on him.

'You're alone here?'

She laughed briefly. 'Three kids, one dog, no husband.'

'Renting?'

'Who'd buy it?' She glanced around the room. 'Due to be demolished, two, three months.'

'Where will you go?'

'Somewhere better.'

He nodded slowly, his eyes wandering. That closed door would be his bedroom. The back door led on to a narrow veranda with a cramped bathroom and toilet. It was all familiar and yet strange. His mother had been standing by that sink (was it the same one after so many years?) with a cloth in her hand. Father was at the back door, shouting. What about? The little boy who was James stood half-hidden by his bedroom door, not understanding the words, but recognising the anger and bitterness in the two faces he wanted to love.

When had he run away, out of the door, down the lane, over the cross-roads, past Miss Petrie's, Mrs March's, deep into the undergrowth where the creek ran strongly after good rains? When had he seen his mother come, eyes red with weeping, to lean against the gum where he and Steve had made a rudimentary tree house? Had it been minutes or hours before Father had arrived, his face suffused with alcoholic rage, his hands bunching into fists, spreading into talons?

'Like a cuppa?' The woman's voice jolted him out of the past. He turned swiftly, almost fearfully, as if she had seen what he had been seeing, had learned things about him that he was only just discovering for himself.

'No. No, thanks. I must go. Thanks—thanks very much!'

He left, and the mocking eyes followed him. He walked quickly. When he came to the creek he stopped, afraid of what he might recall. A pleasant breeze was lifting the leaves; there was 'his' tree, filled with sunlight almost as he remembered it; there was the water bubbling over a rocky patch, catching glints of sun and throwing them up against dark trunks.

And there was the shadow of his father, a darker patch among the trees; and his mother, staring upwards, seeing the frantic fingers reaching out for her. And the boy James was there too, up above, his face hidden behind his hands, so that he never saw what happened below him. When he did look down, Mother was lying strangely, her hair rippling in the water, her face obscured. Father was gone.

They began their travels soon afterwards. He missed Steve, sometimes more than he missed his mother. Steve had been just one of the deprivations. Miss Cooper had said, 'Don't worry, James. It's not your fault.' But something had been wrong. Someone must have been responsible.

Weeds at the edge of the creek rippled like his mother's hair. After a long moment James turned away. Whatever had happened on that far-off day, it couldn't be important now. If his father had killed her deliberately, what difference did it make to him, James, well-off, comfortable in his big house, pleasantly married, father of two lively children? If he had struck her in a fury and left her to drown . . . ? He shook his head angrily.

His watch said that he had spent nearly two hours on this journey into the past. It was enough. At the garage the mechanic was making approving pats with his oily rag at the car's gleaming bonnet. James paid the bill, bought a can of lemon from the cooler.

'Been looking round the place?' the mechanic asked. James nodded. 'Been here before?'

James opened the car door and climbed in. 'A long time ago. A very long time ago.'

The man rubbed a spot on the door handle. 'Not much ever changes in Burton's Mill,' he said comfortably.

James glanced at the name over the garage. 'S. Marple, motor mechanic'. 'Steve?' he said casually and the man nodded, mildly curious.

'Do I know you?'

James regarded him for a moment. 'I doubt it,' he said, and started the engine.

ONE DAY AT A TIME

It is something that any so-called civilised country should be ashamed of—that there are people who live on the streets because they are homeless. It is perhaps possible to comprehend that some people do not want to live as the rest of us do, in comfort and warmth. But there are so many that are there through no real fault of their own: they may have mental problems, or families that don't care. They may be entirely alone in the world, unable to make things work for them the way most of us do, or they may be temporarily without roots and hoping for better things to come.

But when many of these folks are young, have lost touch with parents, are on drugs from choice or because they feel totally hopeless, we should all feel shame. How can this happen in an affluent country like Australia—or Britain—or America? Where are our priorities?

And what is the answer? Probably not the one that the woman in this story tried. But God bless her for making the effort.

ONE DAY AT A TIME

She had always been the same. Never thought things through. Went off at a tangent, had a flash of inspiration, but never saw beyond that moment of perfection to all the snags, all the tedium of nitty-gritty detail.

It was like that when she was a child. No amount of warnings from her mother or from Auntie Glad ever made her stop for that brief space when the hazards would show themselves; and now, fifty years later, she hadn't changed.

Thus, a brief affair with a wounded hero of the Korean War had fallen by the wayside; a job as nursemaid in a well-to-do family had failed dismally; the attempt to be a receptionist in a lawyer's office never even got off the ground. The lawyer had taken one look at her and shaken his head, kindly but firmly.

Now she washed up in a grimy scullery at the back of a small and vaguely unsavoury restaurant in a nondescript back street in the city. Her grim sense of humour accepted it as appropriate. Charlie, the boss, paid her for the week, out of his pocket into her hand so that the pension people wouldn't find out. She started at seven in the evening, finished at midnight with hands soggy and wrinkled. She refused to wear rubber gloves.

'Y'ought to take care,' Charlie sometimes said, locking the door behind her. 'Drongos out there this time o' night. A woman on her own? Asking for it!' But he never offered to escort her through the midnight jungle.

Down the street, out into the mall where the lights were bright, past the shifty-eyed kids dragging on their cigarettes—or worse—past the old men with blank faces and bottles clutched

17

in hands nearly lifeless. She went by them, looking ahead, seeing nothing because she had seen it all so many times. Over the cross-roads, down into the narrow side road that led to the alley where she lived.

Because she was part of the strange late-night crowd no one ever bothered her. The stumping, bunioned walk, the aggressive chin, emphasised by badly-made dentures, the hair cut short, uneven where she couldn't see at the back, not sandy, not ginger, not grey—all of it proclaimed a kind of contained, proud poverty. Her walk home was invariably without incident.

Then it occurred to her, one cold evening, that one of the sleeping bundles that lay in patches of shadow just off the mall was a boy. Young, with a sheet of cardboard under him and a black windcheater pulled up over his head. Why she noticed him she could not have said, but once it had happened she found herself looking out for him. He was there most nights. About fifteen, she'd have guessed. Not much more.

A sudden rush of irritated impulsiveness hit her on a night when the stars were splintered ice and the wind brought a shiver right under her Good Sam's winter coat. She stopped and stared down at him, violating the night-time creed of 'never make eye-contact'.

'Why don't you pack up and go home, sonny?'

He was surprised. He stared back, seeing the belligerent little figure with flat, knobbly shoes and nondescript hair caught back with a child's plastic hair clip.

'Mind your own business, granny,' he said, and closed his eyes again.

She stumped away, the moment passing. But the next night she stopped again. A fine drizzle was falling. 'Y'oughta be somewhere warm,' she said, accusingly. 'Kid like you! Go home!'

'Get knotted!' he said, or some such elegant phrase. He looked out from under the hood of his windcheater. 'What's it to do with you, grandma?'

She put up with it for a week. One night, when the wind blew off the sea and stirred the battered newspapers that had settled for the night under benches and in doorways, the bubble of irritation burst.

'What's the matter with you?' she said, hands on hips and eyes full of malignant fury. 'Young layabout! All your life ahead of you! Get up and make something of yourself!'

The boy's eyes widened, then narrowed with the instinctive self-protection of the streets, a primitive warning to take care.

'What, at midnight? Do us a favour!' And he lowered the hood to cover his face. The anger flared in her.

'You're coming home with me!' (A little voice in her head said *'You'll regret this'*). His face reappeared, thin, peaked with cold, alarmed.

'Do what? You're mad, y'old bat!'

'You don't have to walk with me. Follow me home.' She took off, hurrying a little because suddenly the brilliant idea was losing focus, turning dark, a cloud spreading to fill her sky. She knew about street kids. You kept clear of them. Some were all right, but you could never tell until too late. Even the cops went about in pairs. The back street and the alley were all at once threatening, strange to her, full of silent menace.

She kept her head down, plodding on with aching feet. He wouldn't come. They lived on the streets because they preferred it that way—that was what she had always believed. Like city rats, they knew every dark corner, every source of sustenance. Outcasts, they were, voluntary outcasts. What did she think she was doing, opening her home to one?

Deliberately, she faced forward. There were no sounds behind, no shuffling feet; her back went into an involuntary nervous spasm at the thought that he might have a knife. Who would miss her? Not even old Charlie! He'd find another washer-up, probably never even wonder why she hadn't turned up for work.

Inside the narrow hallway she stopped, shutting the door and leaning back on it, her heart thudding furiously. That was the last impulsive thing she would do! This time she would learn the lesson. In future, think first, act later.

'But I *told* him to follow me,' she muttered to herself. 'I *told* him. And if he did—and if the door's closed—he might . . . ' What might he do? Smash his way in? Strangle her? She gave a little moan. 'I'll have to open it. It's my own fault. But I'll have to.'

She was at the stove when she heard him come in. She sensed him standing inside the door, felt his movements as he stared about him. There was a thin tartan rug on the kitchen stool and she picked it up, held it defensively in front of her.

He was in the middle of the front room, poised for flight like a threatened animal. She tossed the rug on to her lumpy old sofa. 'You can sleep there.'

His eyes were on her; she could feel them. But she wouldn't look at him. She hesitated, then turned quickly, feeling foolish, and went back to the stove. The kettle was boiling, and she made her nightly cup of Bonox and then—not sure if it was the right thing to do—took out another mug and made one for the boy.

'Bonox,' she said. 'Hot! Take care, now.'

Up in the bedroom she could hear every movement from the room below. The sudden scrape as he picked up the mug, the slight clatter when he put it down. The protesting creaks as he lay down on the sofa. She sat on the edge of her bed, her ears tuned for a sly noise, for a foot on the stairs. Gradually her heart-beat slowed; before climbing into bed she slid a chair under the door-knob. At least she would have warning.

It was difficult to sleep, especially with her handbag tucked against her side, under the covers. You didn't take chances with street kids.

But sleep came, and sudden awakening as sunbeams fell across her. She sat bolt upright, not remembering immediately why she was apprehensive. When she crept down the stairs the sofa was empty, the rug folded; the boy had gone. She looked around; what had he taken?

With her faith somewhat restored she ate breakfast. Nothing was missing. He might never have been there. She put more sugar in her tea—a kind of celebration for having come safely through the night. 'I'll be more careful another time,' she said to herself. 'This time I was lucky.'

That night she kept her eyes averted, managing to see very little of the midnight scene. Then she came to the boy's corner, and somehow she had to take a quick peek, hoping he might be asleep. Of course, he wasn't. He was peering back at her, and she could almost recognise in his face the same hesitancy and doubt she felt within herself. She stopped, began to speak, took a couple of steps away from him. And then, without meaning to, she said, 'Oh, come on, then!' and hurried on, her aching feet unfelt in her confusion of sensations.

Once had been enough to establish a ritual. The door left ajar, rug thrown on the sofa, hot Bonox—and then the chair back under her bedroom door-knob, just in case.

The third night he stared at her, his eyes still suspicious, as she produced the hot drink. 'Why?' he demanded. 'Why me, granny?'

She shrugged. 'Don't ask me! Softening of the brain.'

He was silent. Then, 'What's your name?'

Her head came up. 'Why?'

He almost grinned. "Cos you're *not* my granny! It's daft not to know.'

'Emily,' she said. 'You can call me Emily.'

'Not 'Mrs'?' He *was* grinning, young larrikin!

'No.' She stopped at the door. 'What do they call you?'

'Ah—you wouldn't want to know. But my *name's* Bill.'

Emily dipped her head, embarrassed. 'Well—g'night—Bill.' She gestured towards the sofa. 'Bit lumpy, that old couch . . . '

'Better than a piece of cardboard!'

She was muttering to herself as she undressed.

'Why? What gets into them, these kids? No discipline, that's what! Want the world to tick their way . . . ' She grunted irritably. 'And what've I landed myself with? A non-paying boarder? He'll have to go—I was mad, crazy . . . '

But she left the door open again the next night.

21

'Why don't you go home?' Emily said. They were sitting at the kitchen table after breakfast.

'Because I don't want to be killed.' Bill finished his cup of tea.

'Don't talk silly! Who'd kill you?'

'My old lady's new husband, that's who.' He said it quite calmly, as if he'd had time to get used to it.

'Made trouble, did you?'

'No way! I was quite pleased—at first. Until he started punching Mum. Then I objected.'

'Well, you would,' Emily said. 'But he wouldn't *kill* you.' She saw his face. 'Would he?'

'I'm not giving him the chance.'

'Why don't you get a job?' They were drinking their nightly Bonox. Bill looked at her.

'Come on, Emily. You know what unemployment's like! Think I haven't tried?' He started making a list on his fingers.

'All right,' she said edgily. 'Don't make a production out of it. So what are you going to do with yourself?'

The silence was long, and she wasn't going to break it. At last he said, 'I'm right out of ideas, Emily,' and his voice was level with the acknowledgement of defeat. Across the table their eyes met. Emily felt hers prick with tears.

'You've got a home here,' she said finally. 'Nice to have you, Bill.'

'Why did you?' he said as they walked home side by side. 'Invite me that first time?' He was a head taller than she, but he walked slowly to match her painful steps.

'*I* don't know,' Emily said. 'Just made me mad, I reckon. The waste! A whole life being wasted. Made me mad!' She caught the grin on his face. 'Why did you come?'

He shrugged. 'Surprised. You went crook at me, and then—*I* don't know. I was just surprised.' Then he peered into her face, and she had to glance up, see him properly. 'You're crazy, Emily, you know that? I might have—well, anything might have happened.'

22

'Garbage!' she said rudely, trying not to remember the chair under the door-knob. 'I could see . . . '

'Crazy! Don't ever do it again. OK?' Then he laughed. Emily liked to hear him laugh. It was a new experience in her life.

There was something different about him. Emily looked up at him suspiciously. 'Cat's been at the cream,' she said. 'What've you been up to?'

'Got you a present.' He produced a packet from his windcheater pocket. 'Go on—open it!'

It was hand cream—quality stuff, perfumed, in a pink jar with a rose-red top. Emily frowned. 'You didn't . . . ?'

'Of *course* I didn't! What, steal it? No way. Good money went on that.'

'Where d'you get the money?'

'Suspicious old bat! Here, sniff it. Ask me no questions, I'll tell you no lies.' She sniffed it. 'I saw your hands.'

Emily looked down at the knobbly, rough, red things. She hated them. 'Take a good few pots of that to put 'em right.' She was embarrassed. 'You shouldn't've.'

'Women!' he said, tossing his head back in disgust. But she saw that he was still grinning. 'Women! They take your money and kick your teeth in!'

'But where *did* you get the money?' The Bonox was almost gone, and she had to know.

'Stacked boxes. All afternoon. Dinkum!'

She nodded slowly. 'Sorry . . . '

He slept in the spare room now. A proper bed. Emily liked having him there; not for the security, so much, but for the closeness of another human being, one (she hoped she had not misread the signs) who cared about her. It was good to take the sheets off the bed, wash them, replace them with others from her sparse store of linen. It was good to buy Bonox twice as often, to need things she hadn't bothered with for herself—a couple of

23

lamb chops (a boy needed meat), a carton of ice cream because he was still a kid at heart.

But at the bottom of it all, as he wound his way into her life, was fear. One day it would stop. One day he would find other companions, take up with a girl, perhaps simply disappear and she would never know where he had gone.

One day—he might look at her and see her for what she was, old, ugly, gnarled, one of life's failures. And then he would go, and she would have no way of holding him.

'Penny for 'em?' Bill was looking across his cup at her. Emily pursed her lips, considering. What *had* she been thinking about?

'Funny old thing, life,' she said.

'You can say that again, grandma!'

If she'd had a phone, the night he didn't come home, she'd have rung all the hospitals, the Salvos, even the police. As it was, she sat up on the sofa till two, then fell asleep on its lumps and bumps, waking with a jolt around five, when dawn was beginning to lighten the sky.

Her fears had been justified, then. Easy come, easy go. Emily ate a piece of dry toast, drank tea until it was nearly cold. She moved between the front window curtains and the kitchen, picking up odd jobs to be done and putting them down uncompleted. It felt as if a light had been turned off suddenly, leaving her groping in an emotional twilight.

When he came in he had a black eye.

'What've you been doing?' she demanded, aggressive, brusque. How dare he frighten her like this?

'Ah, come on, Emily . . . ' He sounded weary to death, his face pale, his eyes blank with something she could not place.

'You been fighting?' She was pouring water into a bowl, finding a clean cloth to bathe him with.

'I've been home.' Emily stared at him. 'I thought I'd give it another chance.'

'Should've told me.'

24

'Not your business!' But there was a gleam of—what? affection? humour?—in the 'good' eye.

'So what happened?'

'He was drunk again. Mum said I could stay, he said over his dead body. I said that would suit everyone. He took a whack at me. Mum screamed, I yelled. He picked up a chair, chucked it at me.' He touched his eye. 'Bad luck, really. Just caught me. He was too far gone to aim properly.'

'What now?'

He was silent while she bathed his face. 'Well, that's it, isn't it? I gave him a chance. Her, too. I'm her kid, you'd think she'd stand up for me.' The expression of pain was not all for his battered eye. He glanced up at her. 'Spare room still free? Haven't rented it out to another no-hoper?' The grin had anxiety.

'One's enough,' she said shortly. 'It's yours as long as you need it.'

Without warning he put his arms around her and pressed his face into her ribs, holding her with a kind of desperation. After a moment of surprise she let her hands fall gently on his head, smoothing his hair, stroking it back from his thin, young forehead. She could not have put into words the feelings running through her, except, at last, to say to herself, 'He's mine now. No one else's!' And the knowledge was good, it filled her with a brief, wild excitement and then settled into a warm glow, satisfying, complete.

'I've been doing a bit of research,' Bill said while she washed the dishes. His eye was almost back to normal. 'I can go back to school. Sort of college, really. For people who didn't finish. What d'you think?'

'My word!' Emily said. 'My word!' She was so thankful she was nearly speechless.

'Is that all?' He grinned. 'Thought you'd be pleased.'

'Pleased? Oh, my word, I'm pleased.'

'Starts next month.' He was all at once shy. 'OK if I stay on with you? I shan't have much money.'

It was OK. It was wonderful. Emily could see herself, somewhere in the future, with people saying, 'And how's your Bill getting on?' 'My Bill,' she would say proudly, 'is going to uni—he's studying to be a—a . . . ' Well, what *was* he going to do? 'Where will it lead?' she asked him.

He shook his head.

'One day at a time, grandma! You don't get more than that.'

He was right, of course. It was how she had always lived.

'Here,' she said, handing him the tea towel, 'don't start thinking you're too big to help with the chores!' and she plunged her red, ugly hands into the soapy water, not letting him see the love in her eyes, or hear the song of joy in her heart.

SOUND SCENTS

This story was specially written for radio, the result of a competition held in WA by the ABC. It was chosen, among others, and I was pleased with the way it sounded. The title came to me first when I was wondering what would make a true radio tale, and I liked the sound of it when spoken aloud—it creates a slightly different meaning from the one you would expect.

Then I had to try to imagine just how it would be if one sense was lost. How would one compensate? I hope I got it at least a bit right.

SOUND SCENTS

W hen my eyes went—once I had got used to the dark—I began to look around in a different sort of way.

And I found that nothing was quite as I had supposed. No one was quite what I had thought them. Perfumes, odours—even real stinks—all new, all different. A new world, in fact.

People are very nice, you know, when it happens. For a while, anyway. Of course, some go on being nice—picking you up when you trip over steps, giving directions, helping you across roads. They do say you get acutely sharpened senses when one sense goes—and it's amazing how much you can tell about people when you can only touch them, hear them, smell them.

The orange tree at the corner is in bloom. I don't think I ever really noticed it, *really* noticed it, before . . . well, *before*. And there's something else, too—petunias? Do petunias have a perfume? A bit peppery, those dark ones. I never liked petunias much. Preferred dahlias. And those huge, shaggy chrysanthemums. My mother-in-law grows petunias. I suppose that's why.

I shouldn't say that, should I? She came at once when she heard about my eyes—gave up everything to run the house for me—and the children. Her compassion—drives me nuts. 'Sit here, dear—Steve, get Cathy a cushion—quiet, children, your mummy wants to rest—oh, dear, Cathy, it's all so—so . . . ' I can hear the tears in her voice. Perpetual tears. Ritual tears.

Steve's coped pretty well, really. For someone who never found the courage to cut loose from his mother's apron-strings, you could say he's been great. But I can sense those odd moments of panic when he surveys the future. There's a tiny wobble in his voice, and there's sweat. He'd die if he knew I knew! Stiff upper lip is Steve.

There's a child sitting on each side of me now. Being *quiet!* Such suffering for a child to keep quiet. I can feel the words, dammed up inside them. Verbal constipation! Jimmy is on my left, Cheryl on my right. I can tell without touching them. Jimmy has that well-used odour, a combination of socks and the faintly fungus smell that comes from handling pet rabbits and burrowing through bush. A boy smell.

Not like Cheryl, who smells of soap and clean hair. Funny, because they both shower every night. But Cheryl has been a little lady since birth.

Odd, you know, that this should have happened to me when it did. A couple of days when everything seemed shrouded in the faintest of mists, then a sudden darkness, the brutal turning off of light, and me, alone, adrift on a black sea with no glimmering stars to guide me.

I think Steve thought I was making it up at first. But how could you make *this* up? How could you go through the endless medical examinations, fooling them all? How could you stand crashing shins into immovable objects, losing your bearings in a house you thought you knew inside out—never seeing your children's darling faces again? No, Steve, this was dinkum. Not a trap. Not a ploy. Life on the dark side of the moon.

I thought life was pretty bleak before. *That* came about through something I smelt, too—someone else's perfume. I was never good at scents—not then, anyway—but I could tell the difference between my floral cologne and this heavy, pungent aroma. And I could tell where it was—on my husband's jacket shoulder.

The bottom fell out of my world. That's how it seemed. I realise now that the whole episode was unimportant, a flea-bite on an elephant. What *was* important was keeping the family together. I should have sat down with him and talked. I should have rendered cogent arguments. What I did was scream.

He went back to his mother! Surely, I thought, that's what I'm supposed to do? Except my mother's dead. Granny shed tears all round, drowning me and my children in *her* grief. I felt lost, betrayed, hostile, angry. Very angry.

Then—this. It was as if my soul-darkness had spread into my body, reaching out through veins and nerve-ends to remove all light from me, the happy-go-lucky one, the one who didn't deserve all this misery, the one the gods loved. Or so I had always thought.

It brought him back—of course. He couldn't have lived with the sideways glances, the whispered accusations. His mother came too. I wanted to say I could manage, but how could I? There's so much to learn when sight has gone.

She changed my soap powder. When I open the linen cupboard the aroma of clean towels is no longer mine—it's hers. The kitchen smells—bacon, cheese, the thin odour of raw eggs—are all hers now. Cheryl's shampoo, the household disinfectant, even the toilet—all hers.

I'm out a lot. A woman calls three times a week and takes me to my classes. It's a whole new existence, healthy, vigorous stuff, no self-pity allowed, no raging against a cruel world. Someone brought freesias the other day and we all had a sniff. Strange—flowers to me have always been sensed through sight and smell. Now I touch them, too. I run fingers over the slim stems, up the backs of leaves where veins stand out like those on grandparents' hands, into and around the petals, often so much stronger than they look—I wonder if I could distinguish flowers simply by their shape and fragility? Orchids would be nice—waxy, shapely, exotic. Sensual. But people don't really like you to mess about with flowers. I can sense the unease. Sometimes I'd like to crush the petals in my hands and smell the perfume soaking into my skin. It would give me as much pleasure as seeing a beautifully arranged bowl—before.

But people don't do that.

We learn so much, three days a week. How to handle our rage. How to use a telephone. How to read with our fingertips. Braille! I'll never master it.

31

The house is quiet and orderly. Steve's mother operates like a fireman's blanket of foam. Explosions of childish wrath are quickly subdued. Steve speaks to me always in a gentle, penitent voice which is both gratifying and maddening. His shoulder has never reeked of exotic perfume since that one catastrophic occasion. And I know it never will again. How *civilised* we all are now!

I wonder if I should put them all out of their misery? Let the kids shriek and yell their way through childhood; let my mother-in-law off the hook of living with a daughter-in-law who resents her; give Steve the opportunity to play the field? (It was Karen at the office—I recognised the perfume when she brought some papers for him to sign).

So—should I tell them? What do *you* think? Should I tell them—that this morning I saw my face, dimly, in the bathroom mirror?

THERE *IS* SOMETHING
AT THE BOTTOM OF
THE GARDEN

I n a previous collection of short stories (*No Time for Pity*) I included a fairy tale for grown-ups, and was surprised that it pleased a number of people. So this is another.

Your husband's away working, you're living in a new area where you don't know anyone, and you really do want to go to the ball. You're not Cinderella, but you know how she must have felt.

Well, it worked for her. And maybe—just maybe . . .

Read on!

THERE *IS* SOMETHING
AT THE BOTTOM OF
THE GARDEN

I wouldn't tell anyone but you. If I tell Jack he'll say I'm crazy. But *you* won't laugh, will you? Because I just have to tell someone.

It was last winter. Midsummer Day in the northern hemisphere—but here? Near enough Christmas in July, I suppose. Jack was away on that endless course he was so excited about. I was all alone. Mum and Dad were on a cruise to Fiji. And I was mad—I'd looked forward for weeks to going to the Midwinter Ball in town.

Why? Just because! Because Jack was always too busy these days for what he called frivolity. Because I was in this town where I hardly knew a soul. You know how it is. If I'd had children I would have got to know young mums. If I'd been good at arty things I'd have joined a club. No jobs available, of course—I'd tried. So I either cycled around the endless new-estate streets, where everyone else was in a car, shooting past too quickly for me even to wave; or I sat at home, waiting for someone to knock on the door.

I suppose I should have done better than that, looking back. Perhaps I was a bit down.

Jack had said, very grudgingly, that he'd think about it—the ball, that is. I don't want you to get the idea that Jack and I have real problems—it's just that he was so single-minded about the wretched course. And I know it wasn't fair of me to complain. He needed the qualifications.

So I said goodbye to him and plunged into routine. Wash up, make the bed, wave a duster at the polished furniture, empty the kitchen bin, take the food scraps to the compost heap at the end of the garden . . .

Well, that's where it all started.

Now, I don't expect you to believe this. It's all true, but it boggles the mind more than somewhat. I tipped the scraps on to the heap, gave it a bit of a stir, then wandered over to the lavender bed where there's a view to the hills over the back fence; as I turned back to the house there was a flicker of movement among the bushes and I glanced down.

My legs went weak. I blinked. There, sitting on a brick, was a—sorry, I have to use the word—a *fairy*!

Not your average fairy. No gauzy wings or drifty tutu. No starry wand. This was a little manikin, not more than six inches tall, dressed in black, with dark-rimmed spectacles that looked too heavy for his minuscule nose. I know! It doesn't sound likely.

What was he doing? He was reading a tiny book, so intently that he obviously hadn't heard my approach. I think he was as alarmed as I was. We stared at each other for a long moment, then he moved as if to hide among the lavender stalks.

I found my voice. 'Don't go!' He hesitated. I said, 'Who are you? *What* are you? What are you doing here?'

He stood for a second, then threw his book on the ground. 'I knew it!' he cried in a tiny voice I had to strain to hear. 'I knew it was too soon.'

'What was too soon?' I parted the lavender stems and entered his little sanctuary.

'Going solo. I told them I'd only mess it up. But they said it was time.'

I sank to the ground. 'Do sit down. I won't hurt you.'

He moved cautiously back to the brick and perched on its edge. *I can't believe I'm doing this*, I thought. *I can't believe I'm sitting in my own back garden talking to a—to a . . .*

'What are you?' I said.

'I'm a fairy.' Said without surprise, as one might say, 'I'm a Scot—American—Chinese.' A fact, nothing more.

'I thought fairies were . . . ' I began carefully.

'Everyone does,' he retorted, reading my thoughts. 'Gauzy wings, frilly skirts! It doesn't follow.'

'I thought male fairies were elves or goblins.'

'Quite different! They're mischief-makers. Fairies only do good.'

'Is that why you're here—to do good?'

'That's what they said. Are you number thirty-two?' I nodded. 'Well, stand by.' He sounded fed-up. 'You're going to have your dearest wish granted. If I can find the right page in the manual.' He riffled through the tiny book.

Typical! I thought. Trust me to get a fairy with an attitude.

'Haven't you done this before?'

'No. I've only assisted. It was very educational, seeing some of the daft things quite sensible people ask for as their dearest wish. I remember . . . '

I didn't want to know. 'How do you do it?'

'You look up the category, then go through a list of possibilities.' He was offensively patient. 'With any luck you hit the right one, chant the spell, sprinkle, and there you are. Dearest wish granted, one happy customer, and a move up for me.'

'Like a—a grade, you mean?'

'Exactly. At the moment I'm a grade five.'

'And what will you be if you give me my dearest wish?'

'Fledged. Grade six—the highest.'

'Does that mean . . . ?'

'Yes.' He was mildly irritated. 'It means I'll get my wings. *If* I get it right.'

I bit my lip. 'What if you get it wrong?'

He shrugged carelessly. 'Them's the breaks!' He seemed quite pleased at the thought.

'But you might . . . '

'Oh, nobody turns people into toads anymore. That's old stuff. No, we're much more sophisticated these days. Besides, we feel we have a role to play in the stabilisation of the human psyche. It's very unstable, you know.'

I was briefly silenced. Then: 'But if you *do* get it wrong...'

He shrugged again. 'I'd have to call home.'

'And someone would—unfrog me?'

'Very likely. Unless you got Merlin on one of his bad days.'

I pondered this. 'What's your name?' I thought it might be as well to know, even if I could only croak it.

'Cobby,' he said. 'Short for Cobweb, of course.'

I laughed, taken by surprise. 'Is there a Mustardseed?'

'Musty? Oh, she's out somewhere dealing with a shrewish wife. *She's* a grade six.'

'How do you deal with a...?'

'We have ways,' he said darkly, 'of making you stop talking.'

He turned a page and sat up straight. 'Now, we'd better get on with this. What is your dearest wish?' He stared up at me through those spectacles that made him look like a very small business executive. 'Try to make it something fairly straight-forward. I'd like to get it right first time.'

Well, I know it sounds silly, but my mind was a blank. Here was this never-to-be-repeated offer, and I couldn't think of anything I desperately wanted. I mean, I wanted to go to the Midwinter Ball, but not without Jack, and he was two hundred kilometres away. And there were other things, too—decent furniture, friends in this wasteland of suburbia, a precious somebody asleep in the cradle in the small front bedroom. But these were not things to off-load onto a trainee wonder-worker. I'd settle for the Ball, with or without Jack.

'I want to go to the Ball,' I said, a bit tremulously.

'Ball,' he said. 'Ball?' He was searching through the index. 'Ball—here it is! Ball, golden. Ball, glass, for witchcraft. Ball, magic, for princesses. Ball...'

'Not that sort of ball. A dance! I want to go to the Midwinter Ball at the Town Hall.'

'Oh! Ball—ball . . . ' His finger ran down the page. 'Right! Ball—for dancing—see page 42.' He turned the pages quickly. 'Here we are! One, coach. Two, horses. Three . . . '

'I don't need them. I just need my husband. I don't want to go on my own.'

'Where is he?'

I told him. 'But . . . '

He waved my objections away. 'Let's see what happens.' I wondered if that was really enough. 'Look, you'll have to kneel down. I can't reach you up there.'

I knelt. He produced a tiny flask, and with an anxious frown began to murmur the words on the page. Taking the top off the flask he reached up and sprinkled the contents on my bowed head. He muttered once more, then gave a deep sigh. 'I hope that was right. I'll be here tomorrow morning, so you can let me know if it worked.'

'Is that all?' I felt let down. No sparkle, no sudden frisson of magic.

'It's all it says here.' He closed the book and stood up. 'I must say, if that's your dearest wish you must lead a very sheltered and comfortable life.'

I hesitated. 'Not my *dearest* wish, perhaps. But you did say keep it simple.'

He gazed into my eyes thoughtfully, then slowly nodded. 'Yes,' he said, smiling suddenly. It lit up his tiny, perfect face. 'That would be a bit more complicated. But I'll see what I can do.'

'What do you mean?'

'I must be off. See you tomorrow.'

'But . . . ' My voice died in my throat. Cobby had gone. Not a puff of wind or a flash of light, but he was no longer there.

Well, what do you do after a visitation like that? I must admit I began to think there was something wrong with me—a brain tumour seemed the most likely. But when I combed my hair I found something sticky where Cobby had sprinkled me. So I sat before my bedroom mirror and willed it all to happen. I *would* go to the Ball—with Jack!

When evening came I bathed and perfumed myself, slipped into my one evening dress (my wedding dress died midnight blue) and put on the sapphire ear-rings Jack had given me on our first anniversary. All the time I was waiting for his key in the lock.

It never came. *I knew it!* I muttered to myself. *I knew that rotten fairy was a fake. That's the last time* . . .

I was so mad that I rang for a taxi, gathered up my evening bag and the silk stole that had been Grandma's, and went off to the Ball in a state of mind that precluded enjoyment.

Alone, I sat by the wall and wished I hadn't come. No one asked me to dance. The band thumped away, mocking me. My ear-rings were pinching. Nobody loved me.

Then I looked across the ballroom; there, standing inside the door, his eyes scanning the dancing couples, was Jack! Cinderella couldn't have flown to her prince more swiftly than I to him.

'Why?' I gasped. 'How?'

'I knew you wanted to come. I took the late afternoon train. Say you're pleased to see me.' Oh, I was, I was!

We had a wonderful night and went home in a dream. 'Good old Cobby!' I whispered as I slipped into sleep. 'Fly high!'

Next morning, after Jack had returned to his course, I went down the garden. Cobby was sitting on the brick, looking nervous.

'Top effort, Cobby!' I said. The anxiety left his face. 'What about the wings?'

'Grade six,' he said. 'Got it first time!'

Well, believe it or not (and I don't suppose you will), suddenly there they were, tiny, just emerging from his shoulders, fluttering a little in the breeze; delicate as those on a dragonfly, shimmering and spreading in the sun.

He tried a few tentative flaps, rising a little way into the air. 'So far, so good,' he said. Then, with a silvery flash, he shot up into the sky and was gone.

Oh boy! What an experience. And that wasn't all. Cobby knew, I'm sure, what my *real* dearest wish was, though it's stretching things a bit far to give him the credit. By Easter there'll be three of us, and we're both thrilled.

THE ROAD TO PERSEPHONE

When you make the decision to go and live in another country you really have little idea what kind of adjustments will be asked of you, if you are to create a satisfactory new life for yourself.

I found the change of scenery both challenging and beautiful, and this story, which is one of a set of three I have called COUNTRY TRIPTYCH (all of which are in this collection), tries to express my attempts to understand the lives and surroundings of those hardy folk whose lifestyles are so different from the ones I had always known.

I wonder if I got close to it.

Ita Buttrose's magazine ITA bought this story in 1993.

THE ROAD TO PERSEPHONE

The road to Persephone Downs is long and straight. Trees soften the glare of the sun, but the wide, undulating land on each side offers no protection to body or spirit. Its sandy, gritty surface holds the tracks of tyres only until wind ruffles them or a new vehicle obliterates the old. But when the rains fall heavily it becomes a quagmire and the mud tracks are deep; the sun bakes them into vicious ridges until, in due time, they are once again reduced to grit and sand.

A long-distance bus passes the end of the road, but once dismounted, left standing while the coach disappears into the sultry distance, one still has many kilometres to cover before the scattering of dwellings which is Persephone Downs comes into view. Wise travellers take no chances, and arrange a pick-up in advance.

Myrtle Padstow, of course, was never wise. She ran her life on a series of impulses, believing that too much planning took the sparkle out of living. In this manner she had found herself holidaying in Penang instead of Bali; had settled for a cookery course rather than the Eng.Lit. she had originally yearned after, and had become briefly engaged to a young guru on his way to India though she had loved the boy next door since she was three. 'Next door' in Persephone Downs was around five kilometres, but that didn't deter Myrtle, even in the earliest days.

Now she stood and watched as the air-conditioned elephant of a bus bounced weightily out of sight, and she drew in a deep breath of country air. The corn, in paddocks reaching as far as one could see, was about as high as a small rabbit's eye, and green as a lady's lawn; the rains had been good. The spring sun was not too hot and somewhere a bird was singing. Myrtle took another breath and bent to pick up her suitcase and a back-pack; the track was long, but someone, she knew, would be along before too many kilometres had been won, and she would ride into Persephone Downs in triumph.

Such is faith, that was exactly how it happened. A utility drew up in a demonic cloud of dust and a weather-beaten face peered out at her.

'Persephone?' he said. (No other settlement lies in that direction, but 'townies' are strange birds much given to losing their way, as any country-dweller knows).

'Yeah,' said Myrtle, heaving her bags into the back and sliding onto a hot, ripped vinyl seat with a sigh of relief. 'Howya goin', Mr Thirkell?'

Bill Thirkell took another look. 'Myrtle Padstow!' he said with the faintest of exclamation marks in his voice.

'The same,' she said, grinning impishly.

'Ooh, ah!' said Thirkell, who had never lost his English north-country accent in sixty years' exile. 'Well, well, well!'

Myrtle was much comforted by this enthusiastic greeting.

'Come to visit your ma?'

'And me dad. How are they?'

'Gradely! Oh, aye, gradely.' He thought deeply for several seconds. 'Yes, I reckon they'll be right glad to see you.'

'That's nice,' said Myrtle, and settled to watch the countryside move past her in erratic but stately manner, governed by Mr Thirkell's highly personal driving style.

Her mother greeted her with little visible emotion. Myrtle gave her a quick squeeze, daringly ignoring the dour expression, knowing instinctively that the inner fire glowed warm even if the stove was cool to the touch.

Mr Padstow was rather more demonstrative, being used to chatting up his cows during milking. Myrtle snuggled into Persephone Downs as if it were a goose-feather quilt.

On the next Saturday there was a bush dance behind the Swagman's Arms, and Myrtle put on her second-best dress and enjoyed every minute of her evening. The ranks of the younger folk were sadly depleted—for every three of the Persephone youngsters who left for opportunities and the bright lights, only one ever returned—but Brian, the Thirkell's grandson and heir, was there, a lumpish if energetic dancer; and at ten, when tomorrow's early risers were thinking of home and bed, there was a buzz of conversation at the gate and in walked David Farden, he who so many years ago had captured Myrtle's infant heart and never let it quite go. He came towards her.

'Myrtle,' he said in a deep, warm voice that could only be an asset to an up-and-coming doctor; 'they told me you had come home.'

Brian, standing beside her, found he could walk away without anyone, including his recent partner, noticing that he had gone.

To have her long romantic dream so wonderfully reciprocated did heady things to Myrtle. For the two weeks he was staying with his parents they were almost inseparable. Then he returned to the city, and the bubble slowly shrank and left her wondering. He rang a couple of times, wrote once, claimed long working hours as his alibi, and seemed rather less desirable at a distance.

Brian stood by hopefully. He developed a stoic calm which quite hid his own yearnings. When Myrtle went picnicking with him on a bright Sunday he was the good fellow, the mate, the big brother; but he didn't miss the abstracted look in her eyes.

For two months she made every excuse for her distant lover. But one day she appeared at the door of Brian's workshop as he was beating a dent out of his car wing.

'Right!' she said without preamble. 'A girl can only take so much! Let's take the day off and go into town.'

Brian swallowed down his tremor of resentment at being so scandalously used, and ignored the evidence around him of so much work in urgent need of completion, against the natural fear that this opportunity might never come his way again. As they drove merrily into the nearest town, ate lunch

45

at the Pioneers' Café and walked by the lazily flowing river, he carefully and with loving guile consolidated his position. By the time they drove home under a cheese-gold moon they were as sweet together as he suspected she had recently been with the good doctor.

Days ran by on golden wheels, and Brian, his sense of timing honed by his passion for Myrtle, popped the question just before he milked his grandfather's cows.

Myrtle stared at him, her face suddenly pale.

'Oh, no. No!' she said, sounding quite scared. 'No, I couldn't possibly.'

Brian stared back. 'Why not? We've had good times together, haven't we?'

'Yes—oh, yes, we have. But . . . '

'But what?'

'I hadn't thought,' she said, a little sadly. 'I'm sorry, Brian. I didn't think.'

'It's him, isn't it?' he said angrily. 'He goes away and forgets you, and I'm left . . . ' He couldn't finish.

'Oh, dear!' Myrtle looked dashed. 'Has he, do you think? Forgotten me, I mean.'

Brian didn't answer. He turned on his heel and strode away to the cows, and if milking was less comfortable for them than usual he can perhaps be forgiven for once.

Persephone Downs watched these goings-on with interest, and when David returned for a long weekend and apparently took up his relationship with Myrtle where he had left it some weeks before they tutted or frowned or nodded sagely according to their affiliations. Myrtle accepted his excuses of overwork and was seldom seen out of his company.

On the second evening she took rather longer than usual to dress for her date, and even her father was aware of a change in the atmosphere, an electric charge which left them all feeling slightly windblown as she clicked out of the house on heels better suited to city streets than to the environs of Persephone. An expensive aura of perfume surrounded her.

'What's she all tarted up for?' her father asked as the door closed.

'She's going to be proposed to.' His wife's lips twitched slightly.

'Proposed? Not that young David?'

'Of course.' There was a short silence full of intense thinking. Mrs Padstow sighed. 'It'll be a good match. She'll make a good doctor's wife.'

'In the city?'

'Of course in the city. He's not going to do his doctoring out here, is he?'

'How long has this been going on?'

His wife glanced at him over the ironing. 'Since she was a baby.'

He turned his head sharply. 'No one told me!'

A flicker of enigmatic emotion crossed Mrs Padstow's controlled face. 'You'd 'a' noticed if she'd been a heifer,' she retorted, and folded the last working shirt. In a rare expression of opinion she said, 'Better for her to be out of here.'

'What's wrong with Persephone?' he asked defensively. 'What's wrong with it, eh?'

His wife was still for a moment, deep in thought. Then: 'Drudgery!' she said, and carried out the ironing before he could get his breath.

Myrtle was home earlier than they had expected, and there was something about her that kept her parents' mouths closed. She kissed them both gently before going to bed and left them staring at each other blankly.

'Well,' said Padstow at last, 'did it take, or what?'

'In her own good time,' Mrs Padstow said. 'She'll tell us in her own good time.' They heard the bedroom door click shut.

'Oh, shivers!' Myrtle said, leaning against the brass bed-rail, her arms clasped around her bent body as if it were stomach rather than heart that was giving her pain.

At sun-up she found Brian tending plants in his shade house. She wasted no time on the preliminaries.

'I'd like to reconsider your offer.' He stared at her, momentarily startled. 'That's if it's still on.'

He nodded speechlessly.

'I've been thinking it all out, pros and cons, everything.' She removed a bug from a leaf and flicked it into eternity. 'And I'd like to accept.'

The silence grew longer than convention could handle. Myrtle glanced around her as if the inside of a shade house was where it was all happening; while Brian swallowed, licked his lips, wiped his mouth with his hand and then tried to speak.

'What—what happened?' he finally achieved.

'Difficult to say,' she answered in a voice that started brightly and ended with a crack. 'Incompatibility, perhaps.'

'Had a row?'

She shook her head. 'Actually, I was just going to say 'yes'—well, *actually*, I opened my mouth to say it—but it came out 'no'.' She gave a damp smile. 'I was as much surprised as he was.'

'So this is—the rebound?' Brian asked perceptively. 'Second-best!'

'No!' Myrtle looked straight at him. 'No, Brian. You know me—for years you've known how impulsive I am. I can't help it. It's a sort of instinct—something outside me that says "go on! Take a punt! You won't regret it!"' She sighed. 'You can only go one way at a time, anyway. You've only one life to live. And I knew what it would be with David.'

'What would it be?' He was getting his senses back. He watched her face, the quick expressions passing like clouds and sunshine on the paddocks on an exhilarating spring day, the sudden brilliance of a summer smile, the occasional warmth of tranquil autumn. 'What would it be, with David?'

She drew a deep breath. 'Doctor's wife, three children, nice, well-behaved dog, big house in the suburbs, parties, important friends—*you* know!'

'And with me?'

She stared at him thoughtfully. 'I don't know,' she said at last. 'Perhaps that's the reason. But—farming, rich today and poor tomorrow. An old farmhouse, mud on the kitchen floor, a hundred kilometres to the nearest proper shops, nothing after grade 7 for the kids, trouble and making-do and working till you drop.' She went to the door, gazing out over the rolling acres. 'And Persephone Downs!'

Brian laughed, restored to equilibrium. 'So you'll marry me for drudgery—and for Persephone! Am I supposed to be flattered?'

Myrtle turned and grinned at him. 'I don't know where you'll find a better offer in this place!'

Three hundred of Persephone Downs' 573 inhabitants turned out for the bush dance after the wedding. The farmyard and the barn resounded to the strains of a bush band while the sun slid slowly away, leaving its imprint on high, delicate clouds tinged with red and gold.

A haze of dust hung over the road as long-distance guests went homeward, and all around for uncomputed miles in every direction the world lay at peace as darkness fell.

'And that's what I love about Persephone Downs,' Myrtle said, taking her husband's hand as the bush band folded its equipment and silently stole away to the keg.

OPEN DAY

A Victorian gentleman whose work I do not know (except for one quotation) wrote a poem called *My Garden*. (He also composed a poem called *The Blackbird*, which goes '*O blackbird, what a boy you are! How you do go it.*')

But the quotation I know is from *My Garden*, and it is: *A garden is a lovesome thing, God wot!* My mother was much given to quoting poetry, and this is a very useful one if you want to comment on a garden. Well expressed, Mr Thomas Edward Brown (1830-1897). Certainly the main character in this story found his garden very lovesome—to the point where . . . well, read on and you'll find out.

OPEN DAY

He stood up slowly, easing his tired back, and stared around him, narrowing his eyes to see what *they* would see as they came through the gate, the beauty he had created for just this moment.

Standing at the front of the garden he regarded it with the eyes of a lover. He'd lost count of how many tons of top-soil he had brought in, the trucks grinding and backing, tipping life-giving earth onto the wide space before the house. He no longer remembered what it had cost him in materials (soil, manure, reticulation, plants) or in man-hours. Man and woman hours, he should say, he supposed, at least in the beginning. Until things began to get a bit tangled, a bit out of control.

But he wouldn't think of that today. Loneliness was one thing he never suffered from, not when the garden was there to be loved. Alone, but not lonely: that's how he always put it to himself. He smiled a little and felt contentment swim through his veins, reassuring, strengthening.

He couldn't recall now just when it had been that he had conceived this great desire to create a garden. Not when he was a boy, certainly. In their back-street with only a small yard suitable for kid's cricket there was nothing to inspire a love for horticulture. They always rented—that was why his dad never bothered with flowers and such.

It might have been when he had met that girl from the other side of town. They were so different; he a skinny lad of nineteen with no visible future, she a doctor's daughter with the university in her sights. It lasted three weeks before she saw the error of her ways and dumped him; but in those three weeks he saw and enjoyed, with a sort of hopeless pleasure, the lovely grounds of her father's big house. He saw what could be done—with money.

When he was working in Lou's broken-down motor mechanic's business (though, to be honest—which Lou wasn't—it wasn't much of a business at all, more an on-going con job) he longed to find enough money to have a real spread of land. Two or three acres, even. That was a thought! To be 'landed'. To have room to move. To have space to make a real garden, a bit like that doctor's, whose daughter's name he could no longer remember.

The public gardens finally set him off. He recalled it now. Rose beds to die for (as they would say these days); massed pansies and petunias, colour-graded from white through to the dark purple that was his especial favourite. Shrubs he had never found a name for, graceful trees that made a backcloth for the formal beds, and for the wilder areas given over to kangaroo paws and other native plants that he had never felt much attracted to.

One day, he told himself, I will have a garden like this. He bought lottery tickets, often more than he could afford. But the lotto gods were unkind; the money slid away in the wrong direction.

Then, when he was nearly thirty-five, after a life both celibate and increasingly reclusive, his moment came. He was working in a hardware store by this time, more respectable but no more conducive to big money. A woman came in one day, short, stocky, with hair that had never been naturally that blonde. She wore old jeans and boots that had seen better days, and her sweater was thin with age and falling into holes.

They got talking, and although he was never at ease with women he found her less than alarming. He had taken a load of shopping home for her, stuff that she couldn't fit into her ute. She invited him in, and over a couple of watered whiskies they found some kind of intimacy.

It was never physical. He was quite proud of that in these days of over-sexed television. But they got on well, and before long it was a once-a-week evening meal in her warm kitchen; within a couple of months she had suggested that he should rent her spare room.

He liked having a friend. It was pleasant to be able to sit together and chat after tea. It was a novelty to him.

Beryl, her name was. Beryl Forrester. She was nearly fifty (or that was what she admitted to), so that was another reason for keeping their friendship purely platonic. He didn't want to get hitched to a woman who would soon be old. He didn't want to get hitched—full stop!

He walked now up the drive to the house. His acres were spread out to his gaze as he came round the side and stopped to glory in the sight. Trim lawns wound their way through small, delightful gardens, where flowers glowed in sweeping beds; a rustic bridge lifted itself over a swift-flowing stream, powered by a generator hidden away among trees. Pools of cool water supported water-lilies or were full of the flashing sunset colours of darting fish.

Dark-leaved trees backed oleanders and hibiscus around a wide sweep of grass. And through an arch of wisteria and jasmine could be seen his pride and joy, the rose garden.

There were seventy separate kinds of roses. Next year he hoped to bring it up to a hundred. The perfume on a still day was heady, superb. He loved his roses with a passion, and knew that in them he had found his reason for living.

Beryl had preferred azaleas. And rhododendrons. And if she had had her way the whole place would have become one big orchard. 'Apples,' she said. 'You can't go wrong with apples.'

But he had put his foot down. Even when she said, 'Look, I do have some input here,' he had ignored her and gone on his way. Though he was, of course, grateful to her for having made the whole thing possible.

One evening before he moved in she had said, 'What do you intend doing with your life?'

'I—I don't know.'

'Come on!' she said, laughing. 'You must have dreams.'

He glanced at her as she sat with one foot on the wood-box, a glass in her hand. 'Yes, I've had dreams. But that's what they are—dreams. You need money for making dreams come true.'

'Tell me, then.'

And he told her. When he had finished she sat up straight and poured herself another drink. 'Sounds like a good dream to me.' She was measuring him with a thoughtful eye. 'I've got a piece of land,' she said at last. 'Want to try it?'

It was that easy. The land lay out of town on a road that led to a couple of farms, and it was untouched. Generous space, good soil, a small weatherboard house, but a huge job to turn it into something better. 'Want to try it?' she said again, while he tried to get his breath.

So they started. The house wasn't much to look at. But the garden! He could have wept with delight when he saw the gentle contours of the land, imagined the trees, the beds of flowers, the water courses that he would put in. They worked together; at her suggestion he did his job half-time so that he could spend every afternoon in the garden. When he objected, she said, 'I've got enough for both of us. Don't let tradition stop you.' He found it surprisingly easy to forget that a man must work etc, when the two of them were shifting mountains of soil together and planning where the pools should go.

It was when they came to the choice of plants that things began to go adrift. Tensions slid like serpents into their garden.

His soul rejoiced in roses. He could lose himself in rose catalogues, as another man might enjoy a girlie magazine. It gave him a thrill to see those perfect, curling petals, the clusters of floribunda, the stately David Austins like crumpled silk, the miniatures gathered in drifts around a pool.

Beryl thought they were too labour-intensive. They agreed to differ. But when they tried to discuss the centrepiece of the whole endeavour they fell out badly. He had created a circular lawn, a ring of neatly clipped grass, with a bare patch in the middle that was awaiting his inspiration.

He thought perhaps a statue would be just the thing. She laughed in his face.

'Statues? Everybody has statues! Why do what everyone else does? Be original.'

He went away to sulk in his garden shed. It was his garden—his great dream, not hers. If she hadn't met him, this land would still have been uncultivated, a bare piece of scrubby bush. She should thank him for having a great design. If he wanted a statue there he would have one, and she knew what she could do. Now and then she would catch him looking at her when he thought she wasn't watching.

'Spooky,' she thought. 'He looks quite spooky.'

He had become an enigma.

She'd brought over a dinner service when he moved into the little house. One of those blue and white ones. She was expecting gratitude, but he wasn't going to keep on thanking her every time a load of mulch or a couple of mugs arrived. He reckoned he was doing enough to create beauty where it had never been before.

When one of the plates dropped from his hands as he was washing up, he suddenly saw the answer to the empty spot that was the source of friction. A mosaic pavement! Bits of pottery, of glass and smooth pebbles, anything that could be set in concrete that was unique, something that no one else had.

He saved the pieces carefully. One day he went to the nearest market and bought up a number of cheap plates and dishes in various colours, and took them home and smashed them into small fragments. He enjoyed the sound of them splintering. He had a large tea chest, the sort that removalists use, and he piled the broken pieces into it and kept it in the garden shed.

Beryl found them. 'A *what*?' she said, half laughing. 'You're going to create a *mosaic*?'

'Why not?'

She stared at him and saw that he was deadly serious. 'Why?' she countered.

'You've never understood,' he said after a pause that cooled the air between them. 'I told you at the beginning—it's my dream.

You said we could do it—but it's *my* dream. It wouldn't have got anywhere without me.'

'I never doubted it,' she said, not liking the look in his eyes. 'But a *mosaic!*' She shrugged. 'Oh, have it your own way. But a nice flower bed would be much better.'

'We've got plenty of flower beds.'

'A pool, then.'

'And pools.'

'What about a fountain?'

'Not there. It's going to be a mosaic.' He stared at her until she shrugged again and turned away. Suddenly he got the feeling that she was wondering how she could get rid of him, and a tremor seized him. Without the garden he would be nothing. She must understand that.

He saw an advertisement in the local paper. '*Open your garden*', it said. He read it with avidity. Some people were opening their gardens to the public. The idea stuck. His garden was almost ready. He'd like to show it off.

He drew up a small poster; took it to the local printer and had fifty done, and put them up around town. When Beryl saw them she was justifiably angry.

'I just think you might have told me. Whose garden is it, anyway? Besides, it's not ready yet. What about that *mosaic?*' She said it with what he interpreted as a sneer.

'It'll be ready,' he said, not letting her see his rage.

'When it's over,' she said, 'we'll have to consider our position, you and I.'

He saw his dream beginning to crumble.

The open day was a success. People he had never seen before came and exclaimed in the most satisfying manner over his industry and imagination. His soul expanded.

In all, he showed more than twenty people, gardening enthusiasts all, over his precious land. And all of them, when they came to his mosaic, gasped and said they'd never seen anything like it.

When they left, he sat on one of the stone benches he had put beside it, and knew that it was the perfect addition to the garden. A veritable rainbow of colours—he had scoured market stalls and shops for miles around for suitable china and glass—it caught the sun's rays and threw back prismatic sparkles in red and green and yellow.

The last two visitors were men in leather jackets who didn't look at all like garden lovers. They stood just inside the gate, staring around them in a thoughtful manner that he found slightly alarming; then he moved forward and greeted them with a smile.

'Detective-sergeant Pratt,' said the taller of the two. 'And this is Detective-constable Jenkins.' They flashed ID cards at him. His heart gave a sudden bounce.

'The proceeds,' he said hastily, 'will go to charity.'

'We are here on another matter,' said the sergeant. 'A missing person.'

He looked from one dour face to the other. 'I don't think I can help you,' he said. His heart bounced again. 'Who is missing?'

'It's been reported that Mrs Beryl Forrester hasn't been seen for several weeks.'

He thought swiftly. 'That's true. I believe she's gone on holiday—family, I think.'

'No members of her family have seen her.' They moved towards the back garden. 'Nice place you've got here. You do the gardening yourself?'

'Yes. Well, Beryl and I—together.'

'But not for a few weeks now?'

'No. Not since she went on holiday.'

'Where was this—holiday?'

'I really don't know. She didn't tell me.' He smiled at them, he hoped winningly. 'Would you like to look round?'

They followed him between the rose beds, through arches and past small, crystal pools. He led them to the centre, where the mosaic was. And, because the sun was in exactly the right place, the lovely pavement sparkled at them in a myriad hues. Even the dour policemen were impressed.

'This must have taken a while to do, sir?'

'About five weeks in all. It's fiddly work.'

'And this garden—it belongs to you?'

He wanted to say, '*Yes, it's mine!*' But these men were taking mental note of everything he said. 'The land is Beryl's. But the inspiration was mine.'

'Then, if anything happened to Mrs Forrester, this would go to her relatives?'

He couldn't think why this had never occurred to him. Did she have relatives? The policeman had mentioned family, hadn't he? He felt the shock like a physical blow. 'I don't know how her property is left.'

There was deep silence between them. Minds were racing. 'This—pavement, sir . . . ?'

'It's a mosaic, officer.'

'This mosaic. When did you make it?'

He smiled. It had been a race against time. But he had won. 'Finished it this morning.' He pointed to a piece of dark red pottery at his feet. 'That was the last one. Ten minutes before the first visitors arrived.'

The silence became oppressive. If this had been an ordinary conversation, he thought, it would have been one of those embarrassing moments when no one can think what to say. But these were policemen, and they were regarding him with expressions difficult to analyse. The unfairness of it all struck him. He could tell what they were thinking—suspicious devils, the police, always expecting something illicit to happen. Couldn't they see what a great work he had created when they looked around them? Didn't they realise that in order to create such a work of art as this beautiful garden had become, some things had to be destroyed? Weeds, for instance. Trees that had grown too big. Flowers that were choking their neighbours.

He turned slowly, taking it all in. She would have spoilt the—the *ambience*, they called it these days. She would have tried to make it in her own image. She had had to go!

'You have to understand,' he said quietly, reasonably, 'that the whole concept was mine. She provided the means, but it would have been nothing without my creative skills. When she tried to change my mind, laughed at my ideas, I—well, you can see that I had to do something about it. Can't you?'

He glanced up at them. They were listening quite courteously, but the atmosphere had changed.

'Go on, sir,' the senior officer said.

'Well, that's all, really. She wouldn't let it go, and then she started talking as if I—as if the garden . . . ' He couldn't go on.

'As if . . . ?'

'As if it was all hers. Not mine at all. That wasn't fair, was it?'

'You would have had to leave?'

'I suppose so.'

'So you took steps . . . ?'

He gave a deep sigh. 'I didn't like doing it. Even with weeds, you don't like to destroy. They are God's creatures, after all.' He became petulant. 'I felt a bit like God, creating all this. And she was going to take it away from me.'

There was a brief pause. Then the sergeant said, 'And where is Mrs Forrester now, sir?'

He looked down at the mosaic. It would never look more beautiful.

'I suppose you'll tear it up,' he said sadly.

ONE MAN'S FUGUE

Now one for the musicians! I make no apology for my rather strange sense of humour, and I'm sure the great minds pictured in this tale will forgive me for any apparent lack of respect. My preference for baroque, classical and romantic music, preferably orchestral and/or choral, has always given me the greatest pleasure; so my hope is that, should any of the great masters be peering over my shoulder as I write, they will have a quiet chuckle.

If not, tough! Once it's in print, it's too late.

ONE MAN'S FUGUE

He's a nice enough bloke. Laurence Beamish. Nothing much out of the ordinary. You'd pass him in the street. He doesn't wear loud bow ties, or bi-coloured shoes. He showers regularly. He's kind to old ladies and animals, holds doors open for pregnant women, never trips up blind men. A nice enough bloke.

Just one thing a bit out of the ordinary about Beamish. He thinks he's the reincarnation of Beethoven.

The knowledge came to him slowly. Laurence found himself in the city in a near-tropical downpour on a Saturday afternoon, and looked for somewhere to shelter. Within scampering distance was a large hall, and outside it a poster: 'Pilkington Bay Youth Orchestra Concert, 3 pm, conductor Ellis Blomfeld'; and below: FREE.

Say no more! It was warm inside, and dry. Beamish sat back, a single-sheet programme in hand, and prepared to nap the hours away.

For a bunch of kids, he thought, they didn't do badly. Pretty good, in fact. He had little to go on in the way of comparison; this was the first 'live' orchestral concert he had attended. He regarded the antics of the conductor, the intense concentration of the students, and the partisan audience: mums, dads and grandparents, with a sprinkling of wriggling youngsters not yet ready for orchestral stardom. Then he let his head droop and closed his eyes and waited for sleep.

But sleep eluded him. When the first piece was over (a shortish thing by some bloke called Handel) there was a flurry of applause and then the conductor took up his stick and made dramatic movements to call his forces to attention; and young Mr B, without warning, out of the blue, totally unexpectedly, entered into an experience which was to change his life.

'It was—it was a revelation,' he said on Monday morning to Sandra, with whom he shared a clerk's desk in a large and characterless office. 'It was like seeing something beautiful for the first time—something you'd never imagined.'

'That's nice,' said Sandra, shifting her chewing gum and turning a page of her magazine.

'It was like being reborn,' Beamish said, staring past his computer, past the ranks of Monday-morning faces, to the distantly seen window. 'If you'd never seen the sky, or trees, or the sea, and then you did—that's what it was like, Sand. Like finding a whole new part of you that you didn't know you'd got.'

'Fancy!' Sandra said, taking out the gum and looking at it thoughtfully.

'It was—as if an angel suddenly landed by Mr Cornish's desk over there, and walked towards me and then stood with his golden book and said, Laurence Beamish—this is your life!'

'Go on!' said Sandra, studying the stars on page 27. 'Ooh goodie, I'm going to meet someone new.'

Beamish regarded her solemnly. 'Probably me, Sand. I feel totally new since Saturday arvo.'

'No, not you, Laurence. It says here, *a romantic newcomer*. Well, you're not exactly romantic, are you, Laurence?'

'I could be.' He was just a little offended. 'I've never had my romantic propensities fully awakened. Not till Saturday afternoon.'

'Go on!' she said again. 'They properly got you going, didn't they? What was it?'

'Beethoven's first symphony,' Beamish said with respect bordering on awe.

'I've heard of him. He wrote that war-time thing, didn't he? *Da-da-da-DUM!* Didn't know he'd done anything else.'

Beamish's week passed in a dream. He went home on Friday evening to the tiny weatherboard house he didn't share with anyone, and stood in front of his record collection. It wasn't particularly large as collections go, But each disc or tape had been chosen with care. Now he wondered why he had ever valued them—rock, pop, rhythm'n'blues, country'n'western, and not a single note by Beethoven

On Saturday morning he went shopping. The girl in the record shop looked as if he'd said a rude word. 'You want classics,' she said, pointing a red-spiked finger at the other department, to which Laurence had never aspired, believing it to be the haunt of middle age, of matrons and vague-minded people who enjoyed boring themselves in their off-duty moments. He sidled in, waiting for someone to redirect him to his proper sphere.

A young man with clever-looking spectacles leaned hopefully on the counter. Laurence, losing control of his Adam's apple, croaked; but a flood of determination carried him on.

'Have you got anything by Beethoven?' He swallowed. (He wasn't absolutely sure of the pronunciation).

The assistant managed not to look too surprised. 'Yes, indeed! What did you have in mind?'

It was more difficult than buying shoes or a tie, Laurence found. He was waved towards ranks of discs; Beethoven, it seemed, had been prolific. He took two CDs, becoming nervous at the abundance of goodies. At home he settled with a couple of tinnies beside him on the floor; he preferred to listen to music cross-legged on a special cushion, in a faintly oriental mode, his back wedged firmly against his lumpy couch. Now he took out his CDs and stared at them, not a little apprehensively; for what if the magic had evaporated, drifted into the stale air in his home, proved to be nothing more than a momentary exhilaration born of a wet afternoon spent in strange surroundings?

But it was all right! He relaxed with the soothing, magical mood of the Moonlight Sonata's opening arpeggios, was briefly shocked then exhilarated when the final movement zapped into him, and sat in a blissful silence when the music stopped. That, he thought, rapt, bemused, was the sort of music he himself, Laurence Victor Beamish, would have written—if he had the ability. It was about then he realised that he shared his initials with the maestro: LVB, Ludwig van Beethoven, Laurence Victor Beamish—Ludwig van Beamish . . . Laurence van Beethoven . . . Ludwig Victor Beethoven . . . He grew a little giddy. Revelations are not things to be taken lightly.

But the coincidence was—well, *was* it coincidence? Wasn't there always a pattern in events, something outside our control, a force greater than ourselves? Had those initials, LVB, opened a mystic door between the here-today and the here-after? Was there, after all (he wondered breathlessly) anything in the theory of reincarnation?

Beamish spent much of his free time in the local library in the week after what he privately called his 'awakening'. There was an elderly book on great composers which told him that Ludwig v. had been born in Bonn, a German town he had vaguely heard of. Bonn! There you are, he thought excitedly; Ludwig van in Bonn; Laurence Victor in Bonnivale, Australia!

A vague recollection of a numerology fad in his teen years led him to experiment with Ludwig's dates. He scribbled on backs of envelopes, incurred the wrath of Mr Cornish, intrigued Sandra, who was a pushover when it came to obscure 'ologies'. 1770—he added the digits, added the sum, emerged with the number six. 1827—18—eight plus one makes nine. Six from nine makes three. So how old was he when he died? Fifty-seven: that's twelve, and one and two make three. It all seemed deeply meaningful.

What about Beamish, though? What did *his* numbers say? He scribbled again, hampered by the fact that since he had no foreknowledge of his own death he could only estimate. But 1986 made 24, and two and four added together came to—six! What else? His address? Eighty-four, Main Avenue. Eight and four? Twelve. One and two? Three! There! Well, it wasn't proof, but to Laurence Victor Beamish it had the smell of truth. Something mystical was linking his life to that other, that very different existence, so long ago, so far away, a strange world of passionate musicianship, of creeping deafness, of eccentricity approaching unbalance. He went out and bought the Pastoral Symphony.

'Getting right into old Ludwig, aren't you?' the young man with the clever glasses said cheerfully.

Beamish ignored the familiarity. He knew Beethoven wouldn't have stood for it.

'Here, Sand,' he said as they went down to the canteen, 'd'you believe in reincarnation?'

'Dunno. I've read about it. There was an article in my mag.' She was peering through the glass at the hot dishes. 'That macaroni cheese doesn't look too bad. Or are you having a sandwich?'

'Because I think . . . '

'Two flat whites,' Sandra said in her posh voice, designed to reinforce the social difference between someone from an upstairs office and a girl in a funny cap behind a counter. 'What you goin' to have, Laurie?'

'You choose.' He took money from his pocket without conscious thought, because his mind was full of the near-conviction that *that*, reincarnation, was the only possible explanation. Sandra steered him to a corner table where he sat obediently and ate a slab of slippery macaroni with a thick topping of almost inedible cheese.

'I've had this dream, you see, Sand. Twice. Beethoven's trying to get through to me. He's looking through this dark glass, and he's tapping, getting really agitated, y'know, trying to tell me something. Sometimes he holds out a pen to me, one o' them feathery ones, as if he wants me to write . . . '

'So?' said Sandra, admiring the flowers painted on her fingernails.

'So what's it all about? Reincarnation. I mean, could I really be . . . ' He stopped. There are some things that cannot be put into words.

Sandra had no such inhibitions. 'Beethoven's reincarnation, you mean? I shouldn't think so. They're usually Indian princesses, aren't they, or witches burnt at the stake? Beethoven?' She stared

65

past him, then shrugged. 'Might be, I s'pose. What you goin' to do about it?'

He gazed down at the congealing pasta. 'If he comes again tonight,' he said in a small voice, but quite firmly, 'then I'll write!'

'Good-oh!' Sandra said, wiping her lips in ladylike fashion. 'Get us another coffee, love.'

When Beethoven appeared, glaring in frantic frustration through the dark dream-window, Beamish leaned forward and with an arm grown immeasurably long unlatched the glass, which fractured into spangles of light before dissipating.

'Good evening,' said Beamish politely.

Beethoven stared about him wildly. 'I appeal to you,' he said, several times, in German (though Beamish knew exactly what he was saying). Then, in guttural English, 'Save ze music, save ze vorld!'

'I regret,' Beamish enunciated carefully, 'that I have no piano.'

Ludwig v. wrung his hands and sat down at a piano which Laurence had somehow missed. It seemed to be too small for him; his knees would not fit under the keyboard. As his visitor slid to the floor and lay there, sobbing gently, Beamish felt a sense of terrible doom spread through the confines of his dream, until his whole body was suffused with the pain of it.

'What can I do?' he heard himself moaning. 'Tell me what to do.'

But now Ludwig was lying on his back, smiling, glowing with delight. 'Remember mittel C,' he said, floating upwards and leaving, head first, through a door big enough for a cathedral. 'Alvays remember mittel C!' And he was gone.

Laurence Victor Beamish spent the rest of the night wrapped in a blanket, sitting by the window. He watched the street lights go out, the moon set, the stars fade. He drank in the dawn, pearly-pink, felt rapture as the morning traffic began to roar and pound past number 84; and eventually, it being Saturday, went shopping and nervously bought himself a book of manuscript paper and a fine pen.

At home (quite forgetting to eat) he sat with pen in hand, paper spread before him, and waited. Somewhere out there, he knew, Beethoven was levitating, ready to pass on all that accumulated knowledge; but nothing came. It was disappointing.

That night, however, when he dreamed again, the master came to him with a smile of satisfaction, and instead of disappearing he drew closer and closer to Beamish until—well, how else could one describe it but to say that Beamish and Beethoven became one, indivisible, interchangeable, a fusion of souls.

On Sunday morning the manuscript paper lay like a promise before him, and the pen in his hand seemed alive. He poised it over a music line and brought it slowly down. There! A dot, a nothing; and yet so full of significance that he felt dizzy. He put another dot next to it, and then another, and by the time his tummy rumbled angrily for its lunch he had filled up pages with dots and marks and instructions, and was feeling as drained as his mentor must have been after he had completed the ninth symphony.

Sandra lost patience with him. 'Can't you talk about nothing else? I'm doing half your work as it is.'

Mr Cornish became quite irate. 'Five errors on one page,' he snarled. 'You are not irreplaceable, you know!'

But he was! He, Beamish, was privy to a mystery so immense that nothing else seemed real. Indian princesses? Burnt witches? His lip curled. Kid's stuff! He looked around the office. What would they say if they knew he was Beethoven? Hey? What would they say then? Peasants, all of them! They were lucky he would even talk to them.

With several books of dots and notes (he had examined music in the shop and knew what it ought to look like), he sat back one day and wondered what he should do with it. He wouldn't know how to go about publishing. What he needed was to hear what he had written. He asked his friend behind the record counter.

'Composing? Didn't know you wrote music.' His expression was somewhere between disbelief and respect, leaning slightly to the former. 'Well, I really don't know . . . '

A customer, a young man with an ear-ring and a T-shirt that proclaimed '*MAKE MUSIC NOT LOVE*', regarded Beamish thoughtfully. 'I can get it played for you. Avant-garde, is it? What's it scored for?'

The composer, confused, flummoxed, hugely embarrassed, mumbled incoherently. It suddenly seemed ludicrous that he should even think of breaking into the esoteric world of music; but the spirit of Beethoven rose suddenly in him, and within the hour he was showing his magnum opus—*Beethoven's* latest magnum opus—to the customer. Tim? Tam? Tom? He couldn't remember. Later, he could only recall the exuberant comments.

'It's great—it's *great*! You've left *space*, you see. There's room for *thinking*, for *meditating!* You've left it deliberately formless—so few composers have the courage. You've given us time to *improvise*, time to *find* ourselves, time to overturn the stylistic conventions, the narrow confines of custom. This is space music, man, music for the space age . . . ' And so on.

'What do you think,' Beamish said cautiously, 'that Beethoven would have thought of it?'

'Beethoven?' said Tim-Tam-Tom. 'Yesterday's fish and chips, man. Strictly earthbound. Not in the same league.'

Beamish felt the first cool breeze blowing on his passion. But he must hold the faith. Beethoven had appeared only last night, holding up a glass of champagne and shouting, in his deaf man's voice, that 'a leetle of vat you fancy does you gute'. It had seemed very meaningful at the time.

They played it to him; a group of young men with funny hair-dos and ear-rings—one of them had them right up the side of his ear *and* a stud in his nose with a red stone like a drop of blood. They had strange instruments which they blew and plucked and bowed, and they sat before his photocopied manuscript like monks before Buddha. Beamish was so excited he could feel his stomach churning.

It was a while before he realised that they were not simply making exploratory sounds. This strange, squawking cacophony was what *he* had written. He searched for anything recognisably

Beethovenian; there was nothing. It was simply a series of noises—grunts, squeaks, unrelated, unrelateable. The sense of disappointment, of sheer betrayal, was vast and unremitting.

When they finished, Tim-Tam-Tom turned to Beamish with a kind of wild euphoria. 'Great, great, *great*, man!' His mates concurred. 'How was it, Laurie, mate? How *was* it?'

Beamish struggled up from his cushion in the corner. 'Well...' he started. 'Well...!' Suddenly he felt infuriated. 'Absolute rubbish, that's how it was! Garbage! A lot of stupid noise.'

T-T-T stared. 'You didn't like it? It didn't blow your mind?'

'It was pathetic.'

'We didn't get the full meaning, perhaps...'

'Full meaning? There *was* no meaning!' Beamish collected the pages and ripped them into shreds. Horror shrivelled the players' faces. 'It was totally meaningless. Rubbish!' He remembered his manners. 'But thanks all the same.'

That night Beethoven sat in a corner of the room, arms resting on knees, head hanging in dejection.

'It was horrible,' Beamish said, and exploded into loud, stifling sobs that threatened to wake him up.

Beethoven moved into the centre of vision and did a slow, stately dance, his feet never touching the ground. He was dressed like Little Lord Fauntleroy, with a huge lace collar that was steadily unravelling.

'You conned me!' Beamish said.

With a toss of his mane Beethoven leapt merrily into the air, and when he descended he was holding the hand of an elderly gentleman in a full-bottomed wig. 'I don't believe you haf met Herr Handel,' he said as they danced together with light-footed grace.

'I've never felt such a fool!' Beamish cried. 'It was like tom-cats fighting.'

Beethoven and Handel winked knowingly at each other. 'One man's fugue is anozzer man's passacaglia,' said Ludwig v. as they disappeared into air, like wisps of morning mist.

'You're very quiet,' Sandra says at morning tea. 'Cat got your tongue?'

'I been thinking.' Laurence Victor Beamish stares like someone roused from a dream. 'Like to go bowling tonight?'

Sandra yawns gently, not to show too much enthusiasm.

'Thought you'd never ask,' she says, and selects a new piece of gum.

REMEMBERING

I suppose one reason why elderly people spend so much time looking back to those earlier memories that the youngsters don't always want to hear about is because they have, at last, so much time available to do it.

And when one is bed-ridden and reliant on other, younger, stronger people for one's comfort, why not look back to the time when youth and vigour were constants in life, when names and places were not like wisps of air, floating past before they can be caught?

Lily's memories can be painful; but now and then she recalls something that warms her heart.

REMEMBERING

Lily Posen carries memories in her mind that is as capacious as grandmother's handbag, even though today she sometimes feels old and grey and tired of thinking. Some are seldom taken out now. They are the ones edged with funereal black. The ones that have demons in uniforms, chimneys releasing smoke from combustible materials that once were people, in some cases people she loved.

So Lily doesn't go there too often in the days when it seems as if memories are all she has left.

She remembers instead—vaguely—a tall, handsome man who asked her for a dance at the community hall when she was a very new 'new chum'. And the other man, neither tall nor handsome, who became her husband.

She remembers the child who lived for two weeks and then left. 'To go back to heaven', Lily would say in her Eastern European voice, once she could speak again. And she recalls with a smile the children who followed, who didn't die and leave her bereft, who grew and prospered, and who still live close by and visit her every week. There is a blessing in knowing one is still loved, and tells herself—sternly, when she begins to feel self-pity. When advancing old age seems too much of a burden.

But chiefly Lily remembers one special summer holiday. She was thirty-five, and the children were past the stage where they could never be let out of her sight. Norman, her husband, had somehow saved enough to pay for her, Joe and Maria to go to the coast for a week. She had been sick, a bad dose of the 'flu, and needed a break. Knowing how hard it was for him to save, she had refused. But he had insisted; and despite his gentle, acquiescent nature, that would always give in rather than stir anger, he wouldn't listen. 'You need it,' he said firmly, and so she packed the bags and took the children on the train—and was thankful.

It was such a new experience, sitting on the beach, watching the slow progress of the tide, in and out, in and out, mesmerising her. New for the children, too, whose holiday times had always been spent on the local playground or, when they were big enough, out in the bush—children could do that then, Lily reminds herself. In the 1950s and '60s there wasn't this fierce fear of dreadful things happening to them. Joe was eleven, already almost as tall as Lily. Maria was nine, independent and feisty. Those were good times. Lily smiles now, feeling again that rush of affection that used to sweep over her when they were little, and needed her.

No one needs her now. That is both a blessing and a bane. She's too tired to want to be needed, anyway. Life has its ways of shaping one for what is to come. And knowing that the world would go on even if one were not in it was a part of growing old—a part that, as a young woman, she could not have accepted with grace, not even having seen the terrible things that had happened in her childhood. She knew better now.

Joe was building a sand-castle when Lily became aware of someone watching her and the children. She turned her head and saw a man, sitting on the beach in clothes that hardly seemed suitable for a holiday—stiff, city clothes they were, and shoes that would never withstand the friction of sand. Beside him was a girl, perhaps fourteen, staring out to sea, lost in her thoughts.

Lily turned away. She was far too comfortable with herself and the children to make seaside friends—though her maternal instincts made her cast another quick glance at the girl. 'She doesn't look as if she's enjoying herself,' she thought, and felt momentarily smug, seeing her own two laughing and playing together with evident delight.

After lunch he was there again. This time the girl was lying on her stomach, reading. Lily caught his eye, and gave him a nod of acknowledgement. That was as far as she was prepared to go. He had removed his tie and unsuitably citified hat, and looked a little more relaxed. He nodded back, and said, 'Nice afternoon.'

'Very nice,' she agreed, and took a magazine from her beach bag.

It was slightly irritating to see him there again the next morning. She had designated this stretch of sand as 'their' beach, and, unreasonable as this was, she wished him away. The girl was staring at Joe and Maria, watching them play in the water's lacy edge, listening to their small shrieks of delight and glancing up at her father, almost as if asking if she might go and play with them. Lily felt a pang of guilt; she should invite the child to come over and join in the fun. Then she thought, 'but she's older than they are, she wouldn't fit in'.

Then Maria solved the problem. 'Come and see what we've found!' she cried, pointing down into a tiny rock pool. And, when the girl pretended not to hear, Maria called again: 'You! Girl! Come and see!'

And so a holiday friendship was fashioned. It was, after all, pleasant to have a grown-up person to talk to while the children played together. It was even more so when the girl, Katy, proved to be an excellent child-minder—which released Lily from perpetually sitting on the sand. There was a café across the beach road, and she and Mr Kingston (after the appropriately cautious introductions) were able to slip away for a half hour and sip coffee while they (still cautiously) found out about each other.

'Do call me Stan,' he said. For a moment Lily felt herself drawing away. But what harm could there be in allowing him to call her Lily? Five more days and she would never see him again. She glanced up as she shyly offered her name, liking his looks, the Irish black hair, the dark eyes, a steady gaze. All at once she wanted to know more about him.

'Katy's mother died last year,' he told her. 'There's just the two of us now.' It was a statement; he didn't seem to be looking for sympathy. 'Are you . . . ?' he lifted his eyebrows questioningly.

'No. We're just having a short holiday. My husband, Norm . . . '
She stopped. She hadn't thought about Norm for hours. 'He thought I needed a break.'

They talked the weather out, the state of the nation, the political situation. They smiled politely, paid for their own coffees, left before the children could miss them. But they met again the following morning, and it seemed natural that they should do so.

Lily had heard about 'whirlwind affairs', and hadn't really believed that a sensible adult person could possibly behave in such a senseless way as to fall in love so meaninglessly. Her 'affair', if that was what it had been, with Norman had been staid, steady, eminently sensible. She was alarmed, taken aback, when she found she was lying in her holiday bed thinking about someone who *wasn't* Norman. Stan—not a name that inspired great passions, surely? But there was something about the eyes.

The children found themselves on the beach earlier each day. Lily despised herself for what she decided were 'teenage' emotions; but she couldn't sleep, and so neither should the children. Not that they minded. And Katy was the very person to make it all seem reasonable—*sensible*. That was a word looming large in these holiday moments.

'You have made this holiday for me,' Stan said on the third day. She didn't tell him (out of a sort of matronly decorum, perhaps) that he had made it for her, too.

'I suppose,' he began on the fourth day. Then: 'No, of course not . . . ' Leaving the way open for her to say, as she did, 'What were you going to say?' And wanting so much, by this time, to know.

'When you go home,' he said hesitantly, 'I wondered if we could—could perhaps . . . ' And she looked straight at him, into those eyes that she so wanted to love, and shook her head.

'It wouldn't be wise.'

'No. That's what I thought. Not wise.' He smiled then. 'But very desirable.'

Four decades later, Lily could still see that smile. When so much of what had happened last week or last year was lost to her—they had told her what it was called, this strange disease that was robbing her of today and leaving her with only the long-ago, but she had forgotten the name—it seemed odd that she could remember a man called Stan, whom she had known only for a week, and then never seen again. These days, she supposed with a sudden frown against the goings-on of young people, her marriage would have been sacrificed for the pleasures and excitement of a new love. At least she could look back across the gathering mists and see that she had done the right thing by Norman. Well, more or less. At least she had never told him.

All at once she remembered Maria, leaning against her shoulder at bedtime, looking up into her face and saying, 'Do you love Mr Kingston, Mama?' Her heart had done a double flip, and she had felt the heat rising in her cheeks. 'Because I do,' said the child, before she could answer. 'I wish he could come and live near us. Because I love Katy, too.'

Oh, to be a child, she had thought then—and thinks it again now, in her nursing home bed. Oh, to be able to say, 'Mr Kingston, I love you!' And not be ashamed if people heard her.

She wonders how it had been. How it could have happened, that Katy sat with the children on that last evening so that she and Stan could go for a walk along the moonlit beach. It was so out of character for her—and for him, too, she surmised. For him to take her hand and hold it, the hand that belonged to Norman, that wore Norman's ring, and then to kiss it, just once, slowly, before letting it go, was surely something they both knew was wrong and dangerous.

With a sense of astonishment she realised that she had never known herself, never admitted to herself that there were untapped depths to her nature, that Norman for all his good-heartedness and reliability had never touched her deeply. Not as Stan did now. As they rounded the end of the beach and found a secluded cove they had not expected, she felt a surge of emotion so strong that for a moment she had to take hold of his arm and stand, rocked by sensations she had never even guessed at.

He took her hands in his and let his eyes hold hers in the moonlight; and drew her gently down onto the moist sand. Lily, in her nursing home bed, closed her eyes and felt once more . . .

The nurse had to speak twice to her. 'My, you *were* having a doze! Have you forgotten about your visitor? Who is it today?'

Lily, still confused, part of her still on the moonlit sand with Stan, stares up at the face she knows but can never put a name to. So silly, this problem with names. But she knows her children's names, and that will do.

'Joe and Maria came last time,' she says.

'That's right—very good!' Such encouragement. Such compliments when she remembers something correctly. Like being a small girl again with a kind teacher.

'So it'll be Charlie this time.'

'Let me do your hair for you. Must make you pretty for Charlie.'

Yes, she thinks, *I must be pretty for Charlie.* Charlie with the Irish black hair. Charlie, the child of her only moment of passion. Charlie, the secret she has hugged to her breast for nearly forty years. It's important to be pretty for Charlie.

THE PERSEPHONE FLYER

This is the second of the Country Triptych stories. Persephone Downs continues to live in tune with the changing seasons of the countryside; Myrtle is married to Brian, and all is well with their little corner of Australia.

Nobody ever expected that this sleepy little town would suddenly become a centre of world news. But that's what happened; and Myrtle was, as always, ready to deal with it all—in her own unique way, of course. There is a historical basis for this story; the re-entry of parts of the American space lab over Western Australia. But I don't think it was ever quite like this.

The tale did quite well for me. It won the Lyndall Haddow Award (FAW) in 1994, and was commended in an Eastern States competition.

THE PERSEPHONE FLYER

Y ou would have to live in Persephone Downs to realise that what might seem to an outsider a wide area of nothing much is in fact a thriving ant-heap of activity.

Myrtle Thirkell (a mouthful, agreed, but she *had* started life as Padstow, and one really can't expect one's husband to change *his* name) knew, after most of a lifetime spent in Persephone, that the good red meat of life was to be found there. Two children she had, as well as husband Brian; and, as far as a lively young woman with a head full of creative ideas can be, she was content.

The months flowed by in Persephone. Whether it would be a memorable season for this farming community depended on the good Lord and His distribution of the weather. The year had been fair-to-middling—solid rains at the sowing, and a good follow-up to settle a crop that everyone hoped would off-set the recent hard times. As far as Myrtle was concerned, the weather had also meant muddy wellies and a perpetually dirty kitchen floor.

But the sun was shining once more. The days were warmer and the winds less biting. Green paddocks had taken the place of last year's brown-burnt hectares, and would be around for quite a while longer. The hibernation was over. It was almost no time until the Spring Dance.

This, of course, was before the satellite chose the skies over Persephone Downs to make its spectacular re-entry.

But before that event which had Persephone placed firmly on the world's TV maps, there was all the flap-and-flurry about the cricket team and their 'away' matches. This was an old story in Persephone; every year someone suggested that there should be a bus available for such community affairs (especially those that wound up in the beer tent) and every year it was shelved, and a long stream of cars and utilities and station wagons followed Grandad Thirkell sedately down country roads to the next dried-up patch glorified by the name of oval or cricket pitch.

'It would be lotsa fun,' someone would say. 'All the local organisations would support it, no sweat!' And one meeting after another nodded and decided it was a bonzer idea—but no one made the final decision to buy.

'Come on,' Myrtle's Brian had said in the bar of the Swagman's Arms after a footy match; 'you gotta admit it—a bus would make a difference.'

'You're talking about real money, mate.'

'I'm talking about getting a committee together to discuss it.'

When it came to the point, there were plenty of things in favour of the bus scheme. The committee was formed. The first meeting took place at the Swagman; the second in the Thirkell homestead. The second meeting achieved more than the first.

Brian was elected chairman, in recognition that they were in his house. Myrtle was elected secretary, because no one else was prepared to write letters and keep the minutes. After some discussion, old Jimmy Hooper, who had once been a bank teller in the city, was appointed treasurer.

'Here's hoping,' said the new chairman, winding up the meeting, 'that Old Jim here will be kept very busy—that's the name of the game. Plenty of dough! For the next six months, the more the better. We don't want this hanging around our necks too long.' Myrtle silently agreed. She was in some doubt about the whole enterprise, not because she suspected its value, but because she knew the way matters went in Persephone. The mad rush of enthusiasm countered by scepticism from well-recognised, self-appointed devil's advocates; the bogging down in mundane planning; the decision to put it in the 'too-hard' basket.

But this time something generated steam. The Spring Dance was designated as the first fund-raiser; and as the couples gathered in the decorated hall (door prize a night for two at the Sheraton) the money began to roll in. Billy and Mary Bone, married just a month, won a raffle (another electric toaster) and Mr and Mrs Castle, vegetarians both, got their just rewards for being the oldest couple there: a side of lamb, freezer-packed, courtesy of Persephone Downs Meat Suppliers. And that was only the beginning. The fun flowed free and so did the money.

'Pretty good effort, I reckon,' Brian said to his Myrtle. 'Got right into the swing.'

'All those leaflets would have to make some difference,' his beloved said, a mite wearily. 'Nearly a thousand dollars!' Jimmy whispered in his dry, thin voice, awed, clutching the metal cashbox passionately to his elderly 'best suit' waistcoat. 'It's what I've always said. You can't beat country folk for generosity.'

'Don't lose it!' Grandad Thirkell broke in, pausing from swinging his lady stiffly round the dance floor. 'It'd be a lynchin' matter, lad!'

The bush band broke off to wet the whistle, and Brian took the floor. 'You've all done a good job. I've got to thank a whole heap of you for decorating the hall. And the ladies have done a beaut job with the catering—as usual.' He paused for applause. 'But the sooner we get this money together and get the bus bought, the sooner we can start using it. So we're sending a hat round.' He waved his own well-battered akubra. 'And I want it to come back full of money! All the loose change you can spare.' He threw in a handful of silver to get it started, and it began its trip around the hall.

Jimmy Hooper counted anxiously. 'Nearly four hundred dollars, Brian,' he said, nodding in amazement. 'I've said it, and I'll say it again—you can't beat country people . . . '

'What do you think?' Brian said that night as he joined Myrtle in their bed. 'Will we make it?'

'Well, we usually do,' she said, taking his head in her arms and pulling the bedclothes over them. Sometime later he emerged, his hair ruffled and an air of satisfaction about him.

'I really meant the fund-raising,' he said. But Myrtle, mother of two, was asleep.

It took nearly five months to get anywhere near the price they would have to find. With about two thousand to go they stuck. Ingenuity had earned money in every conceivable manner, but now it was becoming a chore, and imagination and the willingness to get involved were running short.

No one would forget the car rally, Persephone-style, when the first vehicle down the track was bogged and thirty cars piled up behind it. Nor the point-to-point, when Fred Ponders lost his hair-piece on an overhanging bough and Simon Coddler thought it was a possum and shot it. Nor the novelty swimming contest in the Thirkell's creek when the Reverend Mr Tonks, entering into the spirit of the thing, skidded down the wet slope and landed in unwonted intimacy on the bare back of his lady organist, Miss Betty Gambold.

But in spite of fun and games, the fact was that by February (with the cricket season receding) the bus remained stubbornly out of reach. Brian wore an abstracted air, suddenly coming out with, 'Why couldn't we . . . ? No, that wouldn't do.' Or 'What if we . . . ? No, the committee'd never agree!'

And Myrtle, between soothing children through summer colds and trying to decide if she was pregnant again or if it was something she'd eaten, tried not to think negatively about buses and cricket matches and money.

Then Fate took a hand, decreeing that one of America's best pieces of space technology should meet its appointed end somewhere in the southern hemisphere.

With so much ocean to fall into it seemed a little capricious that it should roar into the sky over Australia's south-west coast and find its resting place in the vicinity of Persephone Downs.

It was mid-afternoon when the farming community, beginning to look forward to taking its boots off and sitting down to tea, heard a rumble like distant thunder and glanced up to see glowing fragments streaking across a distant navy-blue cloud to the west. It all happened too fast for thinking, but recollections were vivid as notes were compared later.

'They were talking about it on the news,' the women told each other over the phone. 'Fancy! We might have been killed in our beds.'

'Bit early for that,' said the men, eaves-dropping. 'Bloody satellite! I'll give 'em satellite! All over my farm—little bits o' this and that.'

One man's crop had been scythed by a large chunk, and someone else lost laying chooks in the barn beyond his homestead. Grandad Thirkell had been chopping down a dead tree.

'Sounded like a bloody shell whizzin' over t'bloody trenches in t'bloody war,' he said in the Swagman, round the stem of his blackened pipe. 'Right skeery it waur,' he added thoughtfully, his Yorkshire accent still ripe.

It was a couple of hours before the meaning of the event dawned on Persephone. First to arrive was a TV news helicopter, which whirled itself to earth on the paddock next to the Swagman.

By eight the next morning other helicopters had arrived, and cars with military and civilian personnel filled the car park and lined Persephone's one short street.

At nine Myrtle had one of her ideas, and some swift and pertinent phone calls had the whole area on the go, washing-up forgotten, chooks unfed, babies left unbathed. Wives waved frantically to husbands in distant paddocks, the Reverend Mr Tonks abandoned his sermon ('take no thought for the morrow'), and the teacher, Joanne Willis, announce that today they would go out of school and search for interesting things in the paddocks and the bush. All Persephone Downs (population 581) joined forces to seek out the fragments which had so fortuitously rained on the little town.

'But why?' said Brian, called away from his tractor. 'I don't understand.'

'Money!' his wife retorted crisply. 'Real money! Compensation money! *American* money!'

'For what?'

She regarded him with wifely patience, which so often conceals wifely irritation. 'Because, dear idiot, they will want all the pieces

85

they can find. So we shall offer them—at a price. After all, they fell on our land—we *could* have been killed.'

He nodded once or twice as the idea blossomed in his mind. 'Cunning little devil, aren't you?'

She smiled enigmatically. 'Trust me!' she said.

They did quite a reasonable deal with the Yanks. TV stations not only publicised their sudden emergence as a news item, but also mentioned the bus fund. And one day, with the population lining the main street—583, since Colleen Bell's twin girls had arrived early—a splendid bus, spanking new and purring like a pussy-cat, slipped gently into town, courtesy of the US President and his red-faced scientists.

Brian drove the committee around the town a couple of times, and then made his way proudly to the barn behind his homestead where, pro tem, the bus would live.

Mr Tonks had torn up his sermon in favour of one on 'the crumbs which fall from the rich man's table'.

The committee stood down and a new one was elected, its responsibility being towards the maintenance, running and upkeep of the 'Persephone Flyer'. And a few days later they gathered outside the Swagman for the first major run—thirty kilometres to Rumble Crossing where the final cricket match of the season was to be played.

The team, with wives and families, sat in self-conscious splendour as they drew away from an admiring crowd drawn to farewell them.

'I've said it before, and I'll say it again,' squeaked ex-treasurer Jimmy Hooper, 'them Yankees are a generous and open-hearted people.'

'Did I do right?' asked Myrtle, settling the children and putting out a hand to Brian. (By now everyone knew it wasn't something she'd eaten).

'Of course you did—as long as it's a boy this time.' He grinned at her fondly.

She stared at him for a moment, then her face cleared. 'I meant the bus, stupid! The money.'

'Oh, that?' He nodded 'Was it your idea?'

She sighed, exasperated. 'The Yanks!' she said. 'The satellite. Selling it back to them.'

He nodded again, absently. He was listening to the engine, ticking over as sweetly as a well-oiled clock.

They won the match, no worries! Afterwards they socialised, because they didn't see the folks as Rumble Crossing that often. And then, proudly, they climbed into the bus for the journey home. The sun had some time ago slipped away into the western trees.

But the day wasn't over. As far as the turn-off to Patrick's Creek, no one could complain. For a couple of kilometres more only the driver and the least somnolent were aware that all was not well up front. But at the point of no return, exactly half-way between the away match and Persephone Downs, a dry cough preceded a sudden cessation of forward motion—and it dawned slowly on the sleepy passengers that there were decisions to be made.

An engine failure? Not exactly. The maintenance committee, in its composite wisdom, had omitted to ensure that the tanks were filled up before leaving for the match.

'It was Tom's job!'

'Never! No one asked *me*.'

'You calling me a liar, mate?'

'I'm calling you bloody inefficient!'

'Perhaps you'd like to step outside and say that again?'

'Glad to, mate! Glad to.'

The night air was chill, and the sheer beauty of the stars went unnoticed by the straggling line of inadvertent pedestrians strung out along the road to Persephone. It was a long way to walk.

GOLB, FRAKISUNS AND MUR

Anyone who has written a short story on a seasonal subject such as Christmas knows that it is not easy to find a new slant on something that has been written about from every conceivable angle. Children, decorations, Christmas pud, dear old Santa Claus himself—what on earth is there left to say?

This is the angle I found. I hope it will appeal especially to parents who remember that precious time when their children's eyes were wide with wonder.

It appeared in ITA magazine.

GOLB, FRAKISUNS AND MUR

I suppose Christmas is what you make of it, really. I wonder what would happen if someone—a magazine, say—asked for people's worst and best Christmas memories. You can imagine some of them: the day Dad walked out and left Mum, the day no one gave me a video game, the day I broke my ankle skating on the ice.

Or, the time my husband gave me undies instead of a power tool, the morning I was given breakfast in bed with a rose on the tray, the afternoon we all went to the park and somehow it was magic.

My best and worst came on the same day when I was six. Mum and Dad gave me a puppy, brown and soft, with that indefinable smell that lingers on the nose. And just before bedtime some asinine drunken twit ran him over and left behind a flattened splodge that had moments before been gambolling happily around my feet.

We hadn't even decided on a name. I'd plumped for Twinkletoes, but Mum and Dad thought Rover or Butch would be more appropriate. A case of adult embarrassment, I've often thought. Twinkletoes was a much better description, but I can see that it's not the sort of name you'd want to call out across a crowded park.

I don't know what started me thinking about Christmases past, except that this year the kids and I will be on our own. Jim has gone to the Antarctic. He'll be gone twelve months. I'm glad for him—it's what he wants. 'I can't wait,' he kept saying. Then he'd add quickly, 'Of course, I shall miss you all terribly . . . ' It's a great chance, one that not many biologists get a crack at.

So we'll be a one-parent family for the Christmas season.

Sometimes family isn't the perfect thing for the festivities . . . Gran came to stay one year—Dad's mother, that is. I was sixteen, and it had never struck me before that grown-ups could be devastatingly unkind to each other. To children, yes! Children bring out the worst in some adults. But to watch Gran systematically destroy my mother—and to see my father doing damn-all about it—really hurt. On Christmas night, after a nervy day when Gran had managed to run little needles of venom into everything Mum did, I suddenly exploded.

'I don't care if you are my grandmother,' I shouted, frightening myself rigid. 'I shall never love you, never!'

Gran, regarding me with all the affection of a rattlesnake viewing a desert mouse, said, 'I always thought that girl should have gone to boarding school,' and took to her bedroom.

I wouldn't apologise. Mum begged me to. I told her to stand up for herself. She told me I didn't understand. I said it didn't take much understanding. She shed a tear. I sniffed. But I didn't apologise. When Gran died she left various little things to my brother, but nothing to me. 'Such vindictiveness,' I said loftily (it was ten years later), 'just proves how right I was.' But I would have liked her diamond and sapphire ring.

This year we had decided to stay at home. We could have gone to Mum. We had an invitation to go to our friends Sally and Bruno. I thought about it. But when I looked around our home—well, all their toys are here, all their clothes. We have a routine.

Besides, I was eight months pregnant. The baby was due in mid-January. I'd been hoping it would be a girl. I love my boys, but three lads aged four, five and six, taken all at once, can now and then remove the gloss from the daily round, the common task. It would be fun to have a daughter.

Everything was organised well ahead of time. My best friend, Pamela, had offered to take the three musketeers—Greg, Brian and

Andy are the names they answer to—while I was producing the little princess to complete the family. We could manage without Jim, we could manage without Mum; we were invincible!

The boys had felt the baby kicking. They were emotionally prepared. *I* was emotionally prepared. But no one was prepared for the princess wanting out before the turkey had started to digest.

I couldn't believe it. The boys intoned, 'But, Mum, you said...' Pamela, almost white-faced at the thought that *her* Christmas (including four grandparents and one great-grandparent) was about to be radically reshaped, gaped at me and whispered, 'Are you *absolutely sure?*'

Suddenly I had become a liability.

When I doubled up with pain on her front doorstep she was sufficiently convinced. Her husband drove me to the hospital; it was almost like one of those TV comedies that rely on misunderstandings.

'Your name, sir?' the admissions nurse asked.

'It's not my baby,' said poor Tom, alarmed.

'You are not the father?'

'No. My friend Jim is the father.'

'And your wife...'

'She's not my wife. My wife's at home with the other children. I'm just the—the taxi-driver.'

'The taxi-driver?' The nurse looked at me, looked at Tom, then looked at me again as I gave a heart-felt moan of anguish. I believe they sorted it out eventually.

Well, it *was* a girl. Stella Noelle! We'd decided on Stella before Jim left. 'Noelle' seemed reasonable in view of the day.

I slept. Bliss! It had been a busy week. Stella Noelle appeared from time to time and I checked out her vital statistics: two arms, two legs, a little round face with two smoky blue eyes that, in a supreme moment of bonding, opened and stared up at me, frowning slightly, as if evaluating the situation she now found herself in. I felt very humble.

There were carols that evening, but I only heard them as if sung by angels at a great distance. Reality was a tough-faced nurse who came in now and then to check me out.

'Christmas! What a day to choose,' I said, hoping to win a smile from her.

'There's always one.' She rearranged my sheets, which I had just managed to get to an enjoyable state of sprawling comfort.

'I suppose you'll hardly see your family,' I tried.

'I don't have a family.'

'Oh . . . '

The next day I felt wonderful. Stella Noelle seemed to have accepted me. My dour nurse seemed less daunting. If only Jim . . . But that would get me nowhere. He had almost cancelled the Antarctic jaunt when we knew I was pregnant. But I had insisted. Twelve months would go like a flash. Bite the bullet, I told myself; worse things happen at sea.

I slept the sleep of the totally contented after lunch. A shuffling of feet made me open my eyes. There, wide-eyed in the doorway, stood my three little wise men, Greg, Brian and Andy, each with a bunch of flowers in one hand, the others held behind their back.

I held out my arms to them, but this was apparently one of life's solemn moments, not to be marred by exhibitions of juvenile exuberance.

'We brought you these,' said Greg, and they thrust out their flowers. I received them gracefully. Three little faces had clearly been scrubbed; three blond heads were neatly combed. Pamela was doing her stuff admirably.

'An' we got something else,' Brian said, holding out his other hand.

Greg, as the oldest, shushed him. 'We learnt about Christmas at school. About why we give presents.' He poked Andy in the back. 'Go on.'

Andy produced a small packet and shoved it at me. I opened it, three pairs of eyes glued to my face. Inside, stuck to a piece of paper with sticky tape, was a gold coin. Under it, in four-year-old's lettering, was the word 'golb'. 'Brian helped me,' Andy said anxiously. I reminded myself to have a word with Brian's teacher about his fully reversible alphabet.

Brian's packet was long and very thin. Opened, it revealed an incense stick. He had made a card with a picture of a house and a pop-eyed sun, and a scarecrow figure which was presumably me. 'Frakisuns', he had written. He scratched his tummy. 'I haven't acshly got any frankincense,' he confessed. 'It's for the baby.'

Greg, his face screwed up with embarrassment, kept his hand behind his back. 'I don't *think* . . . ' he said, and stopped.

I looked at him. Just like his father! Gee, I love these kids. He handed me his gift. Carefully I removed the tape and flattened the wrapping paper. Inside was a spring of parsley. Greg's card simply said 'mur'.

'I don't really know what myrrh is,' he said, low so the others shouldn't hear. 'But Pamela thought parsley would do instead. It's from her garden.'

I sat like a queen in my hospital bed and regarded my sons. 'They're lovely presents, kids. Give them to the baby.' I watched their rapt faces as they bent over their sister.

Pamela appeared behind a huge bunch of flowers. 'Pamela, you shouldn't have!'

'I didn't. These are from Jim. All arranged before he left.'

I could have cried then. But my tough nurse came in, surveyed my floral bower and, I think, sniffed. 'Somebody loves you!' she said, and perhaps her eye was a little less frosty.

'It looks like it.' I saved my tears for later.

'Come on, boys.' Pamela rounded up her flock, and they kissed me solemnly, in line.

At the door Andy turned to wave. 'Pity it was a girl,' he commiserated.

I grinned at him. Yawned. Stella Noelle snuffled in her crib. Best Christmas? You bet!

POTAGE

I really don't know why I enjoy writing stories about France. It's not as if I ever lived there. But from the all too brief holidays spent there I got a sort of feeling for the place—which, let's face it, is not much like England. Architecture, climate and the people themselves all make it very clear that crossing that narrow band of water between the two countries has taken you into a different world.

Whether that world is to your liking is up to you. I simply find it a good source of ideas for short stories. And I apologise to any citizen of La Belle France who is offended by my tales. Just imagine that it is somewhere quite different, Madame, a place outside one's experience.

In this case, the title of La Belle France is not quite as accurate as one would wish. It takes place initially during the Second World War—a good time not to be in that country.

POTAGE

The war really ended for Marie-Thérèse when Philip Philipson the second came staggering into the village after a forced landing in a field some miles away. After all the terrible years of frustration and anger and nothing to look forward to: after the chaotic advances and retreats, and the unending background music of rumbling tanks and stammering rifle fire—at last, tending Philip's wounds and soothing his homesickness, Marie-Thérèse was able to believe that there was, indeed, a future to be lived.

He stayed, hidden in the attic, for over a week; and at the end of the week the situation resolved itself, and the Allies swarmed through the village in grim thousands, bound for Berlin. Philip, strength renewed, bade Marie-Thérèse a tender farewell, and limped slowly and despondently down the main street to the nearest Allied position. She watched him from the attic window as he went, not looking round. Her eyes were blinded with tears, but her heart was full of hope for the days ahead.

At about the time that she realised he had left her more than memories, Philip was making his last flight; and before their son was born he was back in America, trying to pick up his life where he had left it three years before.

Marie-Thérèse was proud and held her head high. For a while her neighbours mocked her, silently or openly; but it was, after all, a village, and she was not the first to fall into maternal sin. By the time the child was sitting up, she and the boy were accepted, though with reservations, by the community.

'He promised he would come,' she said if challenged. 'And he is honourable. He will come.'

'He is a soldier,' the women said, and cackled a little.

'He is a gentleman,' Marie-Thérèse said softly, remembering his hands, well-kept in spite of military duties, his gentle eyes staring into hers in the dim light of the attic, his strong body, firm and muscular, the blond head no higher than her own, for he was not tall. He was so different from the men who lived around her, from gross Uncle Pierre with the coarse laugh and stories that no woman was allowed to hear; from old Monsieur Raoul who spat a great deal and had a reputation for lechery that had spread through the countryside in his youth, and was still kept alive today.

'He will come back,' she said confidently, and tended the child.

Young Philipe was nothing like his father. He was a dark boy, with features and colouring like his mother, and it was as well that it was so, for people were able to forget, in time, that he was of American parentage.

Marie-Thérèse grew proud and gracious as the years went by. She opened a small restaurant and employed Uncle Pierre's idiot daughter to help her in the kitchen; and she made a reasonable living.

Her thirtieth birthday went by, and the boy was nearly ten. Thirty-five came and went, and Philipe began to cast his eyes around the young girls in the neighbourhood. He knew the basic facts of his parentage, but his mother was not the woman to reveal the deeper, tenderer moments that had led to his existence. These she relived in her own mind in the late evenings when the chores were done and the idiot Françoise had giggled her way back to her father's house.

'You should marry,' people said from time to time, but she shook her head.

'He swore he would come,' she said. 'And I promised to wait . . .'

'You will wait for me, Marie-Thérèse?' he had whispered. 'You won't forget me?'

'How could I forget?' she asked him, melting with love. 'I will wait forever.'

'Not forever, dearest,' he had said. 'As soon as I get back to the States I shall make arrangements to bring you over.'

She had wondered as he said it what it would be like to leave the vine-clad walls, the pink-stone houses and warm, earthy folk of her village; to go as an alien, taken from the safety of her own heritage into the chromium falseness of the American city. She had been to the cinema; she knew that America was full of gangsters, and of thin, elegant women in clinging satin dresses that made Monsieur Raoul's rheumy old eyes pop out of his head. She wondered how it would feel to wear one of those revealing dresses; then she knew that she could do anything, anything at all, if it meant spending the rest of her life with Philipe.

By the time she was forty, Marie-Thérèse was accepted as something of an eccentric. An excellent cook (with a reputation for the most delicious soups swimming in cream and butter), a superb housewife and mother, she was beyond reproach. But only eccentricity could explain how a woman in her forties could still await the return of her lover whom she had known for a brief seven days when she was twenty-one.

She was out at the back of the house, feeding the hens that provided her with the eggs for the incomparable soufflés and omelettes, when Monsieur Raoul's heavy, shuffling tread could be heard in unaccustomed agitation as he almost ran from the nearby bar.

'Marie-Thérèse!' he called, puffing. 'Marie-Thérèse! He is here!'

'Who is here, monsieur?' she enquired calmly, throwing a last handful to the scratching birds.

The old man stood against the corner of the house, his hand pressed to his heart. '*He* is here!' He took out a handkerchief to mop his wet brow. 'The American! The great lover! Philip Philipson the second!'

Marie-Thérèse stood without moving. She felt the courtyard and the warm pink walls of the house swim gently around her; then she pulled herself upright and closed the gate on the hen-coop.

'You are teasing me,' she said without expression.

'No, indeed,' the old man said. 'May I sit down?' He sank onto a low stone seat. 'No, no indeed!' He leaned forward and pointed at her with a thick, discoloured finger. 'The American has indeed come, back to the village, driving his great American car, vroum-vroum!' He pretended to turn a driving wheel, and then slapped his knee and choked with laughter. 'Monsieur Philipson is a very rich man, I think.' He chuckled again and wiped his blood-shot eyes. She was standing very still, staring at him.

'Something is amusing?' she said with icy coldness, and he stopped, sighing asthmatically.

'He has taken a room at the hotel.' He turned his thick palms upwards and shrugged. 'The largest room, that which is reserved for newly-weds. He throws money about like leaves in autumn.' He measured her reactions with a wicked eye. 'Many cases are in the car, and Jean-Paul is even now carrying them into the bridal suite.' He chuckled again, then screwed his face into mournful lines. 'The American has returned, as you said, Marie-Thérèse—with his wife!'

Her face shivered slightly, then was still. Only her eyes showed any feelings, and Monsieur Raoul stood up stiffly and backed out of the courtyard when he saw how she looked. She saw nothing but the beautiful young man who had loved her and left her when she was most vulnerable; she saw the expression of love in his eyes, the dejection in his shoulders as he departed, the last moment as he turned the corner and went out of her life.

She realised suddenly that she was no longer the girl she had been then, that she was old enough to be a grandmother; and she grew cold and very frightened.

Of course he was married! She hadn't really expected that he would remain faithful to her memory for a quarter of a century—had she?

'What is the American's wife like?' she asked Françoise that evening, and the girl giggled.

98

'She is thin, like a pole. And she has yellow hair like hay twisted up in tight curls, and a mouth like a thin red line. She talks very high and hard.' Françoise giggled again. 'She is not beautiful.'

Marie-Thérèse pulled her lips in, in a kind of sterile satisfaction. She waited for Philip Philipson the second to come to her, and she waited with pride and a great dignity that was almost beauty. She served her soups and coqs-au-vin and made omelettes with a superb grace and a warmth in her smooth cheeks. The village was proud and appreciative of her bearing, and awaited results with impatience.

Reports came in, but it was not until the third evening that she glanced through the window and saw the Americans strolling down the road and into her tiny restaurant. She knew who they were because there was no one else they could be; but she stood stiffly, holding onto the door post while she fought down a sense of shock and disappointment. The woman was just as Françoise had described her; but the man . . . ! Could this be Philip, her Philip who had lain in her arms and made such beautiful professions of love? This squat, heavy man, with the thick fingers laden with showy rings? This slightly bald man, whose eyes were pouchy and whose stomach swelled richly but unenticingly? *Where,* she asked herself desperately, *was her lover?*

'Here, Sharon,' Philip said, pointing to a table. 'Let's sit here where we can see out the window.' Even the voice had gone, soaked in rich wines and coarsened with too many cigars.

'Now, Phil, honey,' said his wife. 'Isn't this just the cutest little caffay?'

Marie-Thérèse moved slowly forward and stood beside them. 'Madame?' she said, holding her hand under her apron. 'Monsieur?'

'We have been told,' said the woman, 'that we cannot leave the village without trying your delectable soup.' She turned to her husband. 'How do you say it in French?'

'No need,' said Marie-Thérèse. 'I speak English a little.'

She turned her eyes slowly to his, but he was reading the menu. Was it possible that he didn't remember her? Had she changed as much as he? What was he doing here, anyway?

As if in answer, the woman turned to her confidentially. 'Mr Philipson,' she said, 'is on a sentimental journey. He was here during the war.'

Marie-Thérèse nodded. 'Oh, yes. We remember him very well.'

Philip's head shot up, and he looked at her for the first time. '*You* remember me?' She regarded him without speaking. He stood up slowly and held out a hand. But she moved back from him.

'*Very* well, monsieur.' She watched his face as he struggled with his memory.

Her son returned from work as she prepared the visitors' meal, and drily she pointed into the dining-room. 'There is your father, son.' Philipe peered through the doorway.

'*That?*' He turned, stared at her. 'That gross man? But you told me . . .'

'All things change.' She added seasonings to the food.

As she stirred, a shadow fell across the kitchen. The American was standing there, hesitant.

'You want something, monsieur?'

'I have been thinking,' he began. 'My memory is not too good—but—isn't it Marie?'

'It is,' she said. 'And this is my son.'

'Your son,' he echoed, holding out his hand to the young man.

'His name is Philipe,' she said, and stirred the soup.

The American was silent for a moment. He seemed to be having trouble with his voice. The young Philipe regarded him with amusement.

'You mean . . . ?'

She nodded. 'Your son,' she said gently. 'Philipe Philipson the third.'

The silence was broken only by the bubbling of the soup.

'Sharon and I,' he said at last, as if breath were being forced out of him, 'have never been able to have children.'

It seemed to Marie-Thérèse that the silence and the bubbling would go on forever.

'Forgive me,' Philipson said. 'It has been a great shock to me.'

He felt in his pocket and regarded his wallet with some doubt. Her eyes snapped with pride and disbelief. 'May I . . . ? After all, there must have been expenses—you have been put to considerable trouble . . . ' he floundered, and she would not help him. He took out a large number of notes, his fingers fumbling through them shakily. 'Please—accept this—from an old friend . . . '

Marie-Thérèse drew herself up and stared coldly at him. Thus do dreams crumble! And then she thought of the day-to-day finances, the constant effort to make do, and she smiled, almost graciously. Stretching out her hand she took the notes, counted them, and put them carefully in her pocket. Her son watched her with astonishment.

'Please, sit down,' she said to the stranger who now lived in her lover's body. 'Your soup is almost ready.' Philip Philipson the second sighed with relief and went back to his wife.

The meal was eaten quickly, and the well-to-do American pair got into their glossy American car and made their way out of the village on their way to Cherbourg and the American way of life. Marie-Thérèse stood by the gate with Philipe's arm around her shoulders.

'You are not angry?' he enquired curiously. 'When you accepted his money I could hardly believe my eyes.'

She was silent for a moment. 'Until he offered me the money,' she said quietly, 'I was in pain for what I had lost. But now . . . ' To her son's astonishment she began to laugh, gently at first, and then she chuckled and began to shake.

'What is funny?' he said. 'Today you are a different woman. Why do you laugh?'

She wiped tears from her eyes with the corner of her apron, then stood with her hands folded in front of her in the typical peasant attitude of all time.

'He had forgotten all about me. For twenty-five years I waited, but he had forgotten. Do you not think that deserves some punishment?' She chuckled again, and Philipe, not knowing why, joined in. They turned and went into the house.

'There is that in the soup,' she said, shaking with merriment, 'that will cause them acute discomfort all the way to Cherbourg!'

Philipe stared at her, and then he shouted with laughter.

'And it is well-known,' he cried, 'that between here and Cherbourg the sanitation is of the most primitive!'

HOW SHALL I KILL HIM?

In terms of 'getting one's own back', this tale probably follows the previous one quite neatly. But *this* young woman appears to lack the dry sense of humour that got Marie-Thérèse through her ordeal. It does seem strange that some women are so deeply attracted to *machismo* that they will make the same mistake over and over again, and end up with disastrous marriages.

This isn't the way to solve the problem.

HOW SHALL I KILL HIM?

Let me count the ways!

Once you've made up your mind to something, there's no going back. It'll sit there in your head, this sudden determination, and no amount of trying will get you back to where you were before the idea struck you.

That's how it was when, slowly, slowly, the idea came to me to kill my husband. The gradual descent from dissatisfaction to anger to hate to bitter resentment takes time, but once there, there's no way out. The idea has taken root, and it comes back to haunt you.

How to do it is another matter. For your average well-behaved middle-class wife, murder is not normally on the agenda. There, I've said it! Murder! It's an ugly, black word. Very suitable, really. Being married to *him* is an ugly, black situation.

So, as the weeks and months went by, I began to compile a list of ways in which I could achieve this dreadful outcome. I took to reading the newspaper with avidity, searching out the different methods used by dissatisfied spouses to remove the source of their dissatisfaction. And some are really weird. Believe me.

In the evenings, while he watched the TV, some goofy footy program full of schoolboy innuendo, or half-dressed girls prancing in front of the cameras, I would bring up on the whiteboard of my mind the means I might employ to—well, to finish him off.

Leaving him was no option. He was too possessive. I knew he would follow me wherever I tried to hide, and you can forget about police protection and all that. People like my husband are not fazed by little details like the police. Thank God—and I often did—that we had never had children.

'Whass'matter? Lost your sense of humour, have you? *You* ought to get one o' those undies things—might make you look a bit less depressing.' That was his idea of conversation. Mine was not to answer him.

I made a list. I was very efficient. If I was going to embark on the ultimate criminal career I wanted it to be done properly. So . . .

One! I could bore him to death with my 'incessant brainless chatter'. Considering how seldom I answered him back, I could never see what justification he had for this accusation. 'Shut up!' he'd say, if I did express an opinion. 'What would you know about it?' And 'Shut up!' if we were out with so-called 'friends'—his, of course, I wasn't allowed friends of my own. 'You gotta forgive her, mate—she's just a big-mouth.' It seems odd to say I got used to it. And to the strange looks his friends would give me, just for a moment, before they got back into the discussion of the latest match or someone's car engine. Bernie, for instance. I could never make out the look on Bernie's face.

So—two! Kill him with kindness. Surely, I thought in my calmer moments, *surely* he would react to the gentle approach. Make his favourite food, see he never ran out of his favourite beer. Not too easy when he had the 'mates' around for the evening. If I showed him how loving, how compassionate I was, wouldn't that make a difference?

No, is the short answer. 'Ger-off!' he'd snarl when I tried to rearrange the cushions on the sofa. And, 'OK, OK, so *last* week I liked Foster's—so *this* week I like . . . ' and I'd find myself in the car, down to the liquor shop, to replenish the already full bar fridge. I would feel Bernie's eyes on me. Was he wondering why I didn't hit back? Why I took it for so long? I don't know.

Three? Poison him with my homemade soup? The trouble was, he didn't really like anything I cooked. Compared everything with what his mother did. She, so he said, could make the cheapest cut of meat taste like the food of the gods. She made sponge cakes

106

that would float off the plate. Always made her own ice cream with REAL cream! And never went too heavy on the vegies. Sadly, I could never confirm this for myself. She died (of food poisoning after eating local mussels) the year before I married her discriminating son.

I suppose, looking back, that I was intended as a sort of replacement in the kitchen. What a shock for him! Our first home-cooked meal—but that's irrelevant. More to the point, how could I induce him to eat my own home-cooked *soup*? Well, I couldn't. That was very clear. I made a really good one, full of interesting ingredients, and popped a bit of snail bait—just a smidgen—into his helping. Just to try.

He took a spoonful, and before his taste-buds had sent the message he threw the spoon down and glared at me. 'What is it? Tastes like rat poison!' Close, I thought. Very close. Cross that off the list.

I made a picnic and suggested we should 'go bush' and have a nice day out. He stared at me as if I was crazy, then suddenly nodded. 'Why not? Might do you good.'

I thought that was a funny way of putting it. But with Plan Four up and running I wasn't going to make waves. We put the gear in the car, filled a big bottle with water, checked that we had the spare tyre fully inflated, and went off, looking, no doubt, like any normal, happy couple on holiday.

We drove up into the hills. It was a perfect day. The clouds were white and fluffy, like cotton wool glued to a clear blue sky. A light breeze, enough to keep us cool in what had been forecast as a fairly hot day. For a few moments I let myself forget Plan Four and simply enjoyed the car's smooth motion and the lovely countryside sweeping past us.

But I needed to be conscious of where we were. There was a track down which we had gone a couple of times when we were in courting mode. I saw it, all at once, and called him to stop. 'Down there!' I said. 'Let's go down there.'

And for once he didn't argue. He turned the car and we moved slowly along the track until we came to the place I had in mind. A small clearing surrounded by thick bush. I knew that a short way through the bush there was a cliff, the remains of a quarry that had briefly existed long year ago. No one went there now, not to cut stone. I was pretty sure we wouldn't be seen.

The bush went right up to the side of the cliff. He would be on the edge before he knew it. If I played my cards right I could tip him over the side, take the car and go for help, and play the demented widow.

I wonder if he suspected something. Do you think I could get him into the bush, away from the car? No! He sat himself down on one of those little beach chairs that we keep in the boot, and waited for me to attend to his every need. So what else was new?

'Wouldn't you like to go for a walk?' I said after we had eaten.

'No. I think I'll have a little nap.' He settled himself in the chair and before I could say anything he was dozing off. I sat and watched him. Asleep, he still had something of the charm for me that had led me into this mess. Why couldn't we make a go of it? Why did he have to be so—so—well, *cruel* was the word that came to mind? What sort of woman would have been able to make him happy? I don't know.

I stood up after a while, bored with my own thoughts. I walked a little away from the car and knew I was going towards the quarry. I didn't want to—that plot had failed—but I couldn't help it. Perhaps the answer was not to try to finish *him* off, but to do away with myself. Perhaps it was all my fault, anyway. I came suddenly through the bushes and stopped just in time to stop myself from sliding over the edge. It was further than I had remembered to the bottom. I peered over very cautiously. Yes, if Plan Four had worked, he would by now be lying dead at the foot of the cliff, and I would be practising my new role as distraught widow. Damn!

I heard him calling. 'Where are you? Where the hell are you?'

Why didn't I answer? I don't remember. This could have been the solution, trip him up, see him roll, bump, fall, *smash* down on those jagged rocks. And I didn't do it. I moved away, back towards the clearing where the car was. Or I thought I did. But I could hear him calling, getting more and more angry, and I couldn't find the clearing. *I couldn't find the damned clearing!*

And then I heard the car driving away. I couldn't believe my ears. *He* had gone and left *me*! It would take ages to find my way out, even if I could find the track. Once get lost in Australia's bush and you are in deep, deep trouble. There's so much of it.

I hoped he had gone to get the SES. Police. Fire service. Anyone! I feared he might have turned the tables on me, seen a good way of getting rid of me and starting over with someone else. Then I thought, no, he enjoys tormenting me too much to let me go. He's got some other thing lined up for me. Perhaps he's going to leave me for an hour or two to 'learn my lesson'. Then he'll 'rescue' me. Then he'll never stop telling his friends (especially Bernie) what a good husband he is, how stupid I am, how he tried to find help but couldn't, how he came back and saw me plodding through the last bit of bush before I reached the track, how I'd promised to be careful in future, because what would he do without me?

And that's how it happened, of course. I was exhausted, dehydrated, miserable when he found me. And he was as derisive, as sarcastic as he had ever been. 'What were you thinking of?' he demanded several times. And I almost told him. But I didn't.

Plan Five was quite simple. I tried to drown him in my tears. My depression welled up on the way home, and I began to cry—unstoppably. He was surprisingly patient about it at first. Probably liked to think he'd got the upper hand once again. But when I had cried all the way home, all through the evening, half the night (until I cried myself to sleep) and most of the next day he got very irritable. So Plan Five joined the previous four. I obviously wasn't intended to get rid of him by subtle means.

I lay in bed and regarded him in the dim illumination from a street light. He *was* good-looking. Was that why I had married him? Or was there something about his masterfulness that had caught me, won me—*trapped* me? I shifted on the pillow, and the thought suddenly came to me: asphyxiation! Perhaps I could hold the pillow over his face for long enough—but no, of course I couldn't. He'd wake up, and he was strong. Strong! Forget that, I told myself. There must be another way.

How about—how about *bashing* him to death? There was a baseball bat in the cupboard, something left over from his sporting youth. I could slip out of bed, get the bat and—hey presto! Merry widowhood.

Only—he would probably wake up, grab the bat, and it would be curtains for me. And anyway, I wouldn't have a leg to stand on in court. There would be no doubt at all that I'd done it. All those eyes, staring at me, knowing that I was a murderess. It wasn't to be borne. DNA testing, my fingerprints on the weapon, forget it! And his mates, well, Bernie specifically, regarding me with disgust. I could bear that, I thought, but I didn't fancy the prison sentence or the columns in the newspapers.

A for asphyxiation. B for bashing. I lay there in the near-dark and stared up at the almost invisible ceiling. Alphabetic murders, I was pondering. How far could I go through the alphabet? C? Cut . . . club . . . chop—chop what? Well, I could chop off his—perhaps not! No, I didn't think I could do that. Blood, and who knows what else? Not that he didn't deserve it.

So on to D. Decapitate came into my mind. A nice round word. Means exactly what it says, but somehow sounds better then 'beheading'. There were good knives in the kitchen, and a chopper in the garage. But the problems were the same as with 'B' and 'C'. All that blood, and everyone knowing what I'd done. Move on to 'E'.

Electrocution! Now, there was a possibility. People do get electrocuted, and often there's no one to blame, only carelessness. I could work something out, surely, that would finish him off and leave me free?

I was up early. I'd slept well after my great decision was made. I went into the kitchen and began to check out all the electric cables. The toaster, microwave oven, kettle, electric frying pan—all their wires were intact. He's meticulous about them. That was the thing I'd forgotten. Perhaps I could get him to change a light globe, and switch the light on while he had his hands . . . no. It would never work. If I cut into one of the cables, perhaps . . . I was getting very dejected about the whole thing. And then he appeared at the door, hair ruffled, eyes still full of sleep.

'Haven't you got the coffee on yet? God, what a lazy bitch you are! Bring me a cup when it's ready. What are you doing with that? You'll electrocute yourself. As if it matters . . . ' And he went off with a guffaw, rubbing the back of his head and very pleased with himself.

'F'? I poured out his coffee and took it to him. My spirits were low. I couldn't think of anything murderous that began with F. Back in the kitchen I came up with 'flog'. But that had the same hazards a 'B' for bash. So—'G'.

There must be murders committed by 'G'. But all I could think of was garrotting. And I wasn't sure how to do it. I wasn't even sure how to spell it. Which brought me to 'H'. And the obvious H-murder would be hanging. I played with the idea while I drank my half-cold coffee and ate a piece of toast from the totally safe toaster. Hanging meant no blood. It could be dressed up to look like suicide—it often was, in crime stories. But there was a clear problem: if he was conscious, there was no way he would let me hang him, and if he was unconscious he would be too heavy for me to drag up at the end of a rope.

There were still 18 letters to go, and some, like Z for example, would be difficult to match with a fatality. Besides, I felt too tired. Too much thinking had made me dizzy. I accepted that murder wasn't the way out. It had been tempting, but I didn't have the kind of mentality that could plan something like that. I had two choices left. Either I could continue to put up with my life—and him—and make the best of it. (Though what the best could be was beyond my comprehension). Or I could leave him, escape, find somewhere that he would never search for me. And that, as I've already said, would be near impossible. Control freaks like my husband don't give up. They can't face the knowledge that someone has beaten them at their own game.

I read that in a magazine somewhere.

I decided to do the washing up.

He was surprisingly chirpy when he got up. 'I feel like going to the sea,' he said, stretching his arms and yawning, as if he was a perfectly normal human being. 'Get your gear together. We'll eat at the café on the beach.'

I stared at him. This was new. Perhaps after all we could make something of this mess we were both in. I scuttled around, getting bathers and sun cream and so on into the big basket we used to use for these outings when things had not become quite so ugly between us.

The ocean was beautiful. Perhaps I was in an exalted state of consciousness or something, because I never remember the sea being so blue-green and translucent, the sky so clear, the sun so welcoming. And I went on feeling like that until another car drew up beside us, and Bernie and two friends got out.

'Hey', he said, 'this was a great idea, mate!' And I realised that my only part in it had been to 'get the gear together'. Suddenly the sea became grey, the sun fiercely angry, the sky a brass bowl of heat.

When we had eaten—or they had, my appetite had gone—I wandered down the little jetty at the end of the beach. The three men were lying on the sand, tinnies in hand and in a big esky behind them, *my* sun cream on their revolting noses. Well, this was the end. I knew when I was beaten. I saw Bernie's eyes on me with that strange expression I had never been able to analyse. Did he like me? Hate me? Feel sorry for me? I had no idea.

I sat on the end of the jetty. The water was deep enough for swimming. I could see the bottom clearly, and a small fish that was circling the wooden support of the jetty like a minuscule shark searching for prey. Prey. That was what I was. His prey. I stopped thinking. Stopped feeling. As I went into the water I was thankful that at last I had made up my mind. This was the only way out. I was a strong swimmer—stronger than he was, and I could get well out before anyone knew what I was doing. Drowning was painful, I had heard, but only for a short time. Just as the water streamed into the lungs. Well, a few moments of pain would be worth it.

As I struck out, still fully dressed, I heard a shout from the shore. One of them had seen me. I glance back and saw him, tearing his shirt off, running along the jetty. He dived in. What had I been thinking of? Of course he wouldn't let me go that easily. I swam faster.

But his male muscles outdid my female ones for those first few minutes. He caught up with me. 'What the hell do you think you're doing?' he spluttered. He grabbed at me. I evaded him and kept swimming. He would tire before I would, I knew that. But he wasn't giving up. Coughing and spluttering, he came up behind me and held on to my foot. I struggled, and he let go as a wave hit him.

Then I stopped swimming. I turned towards him and let myself sink into the water until my head was covered. I flapped around and felt his hand on my arm. Waiting for a long half minute, I broke through into the air and took a lungful before sinking again, making a great disturbance as I went. I swam a little way away, under water, and waited for him to catch me. And as he grabbed my hair I dived for his legs. And held on, pulling him down until his head was under water.

He'd never been keen on getting his head under, always preferring to keep near the surface. I felt his legs kicking, desperately trying to get to air, but I held on grimly, hoping he would give in before I ran out of breath. And he did. I came up, letting his legs go, and holding his shoulders tightly, his head still under water. Dimly I was aware of commotion on the beach. People were running. Somebody screamed. I looked down at him and I knew it was over.

They pulled me out of the water. I was barely conscious myself, though with stress rather than drowning. I was blubbing like a baby, shaking like a leaf. 'I killed him! I killed him!' I kept saying through shuddering lips. I could hear myself, but I couldn't stop. 'I killed him!'

'No,' they said. 'No, you didn't.'

'I did. I did! I killed him.'

But they were adamant and oh, so kind. 'No. He saw you struggling, and jumped in to save you. He was very brave.'

'I killed him,' I whispered as they got me into the ambulance.

The driver shook his head. 'He tried to save you. Relax! Here . . . ' and he put the oxygen mask over my face and went to the driver's seat.

'I killed him,' I said piteously to the nurse in casualty.

'Now, you mustn't think like that,' she said, holding my wrist and timing my pulse.

So I didn't. And life is so pleasant without him that I wonder why it took me so long.

Only an odd look in Bernie's bloodshot eyes makes me stop and think, now and then. He's being nice to me. Too nice.

SPRING CROP

Another one from La Belle France. But whichever country one is born in, it doesn't do to stand out from the crowd. There seems to be an inbuilt barrier, perhaps left over from the cave days, to destroy what one does not understand. It may have been a safety factor at some long-distant historical time—but shouldn't we have got over it by now? Well, François did—in his own way.

SPRING CROP

Maria made a vow in those first few weeks after her son François was born. As she bent over his cradle, watching the tiny, delicate hands clasp and unclasp, the small mouth widening into passionate demands for food, the smooth-olive skin of the heart-shaped face, she promised herself—and the baby—that there would be something better for him in life than the day-by-day struggles of a village peasant.

As the baby grew, her promise became a passion. There was a fine quality in his little face that was seldom seen among the village boys, a quality of gentleness and caring that she found irresistible. However hard it might be, whatever the hurdles to be overcome, Maria maintained a single-mindedness that would not be sidetracked by the jibes of friends or the sneers of enemies.

'Ho!' her own mother would call at her from the smoke-filled cottage by the river. 'And how is our little one today? Still drinking up his milk and brushing his curls, hey?' Maria tossed her head and stalked by, her nose in the air. They would laugh now, but wait until the child was grown and—and President, perhaps! Or famous star of the screen appearing in the nearby city with golden girls on every hand, far different from the dark and swarthy maidens surrounding him here in the village. There was nothing here—nothing for a slim, attractive child who turned his mother's heart in her breast every time she looked at him. Here was only living death, hemmed in on every side by ox-like men of the soil, and gipsy-dark women and girls who, soon enough, learned to put away from them forever any dreams they may once have had of romance, beauty, glamour.

117

Men who spent their days mating cattle, scraping a hard living from the thin, boulder-strewn soil that, often enough, killed them with despair and frustration—men like these were not expected to perform as great lovers, with the smooth charm of a Chevalier or the disturbingly seductive air of a Hollywood star.

When he was thirteen, François came home with a bloody nose. He seemed calm enough, almost detached.

'They were laughing at me,' he said in answer to his mother's query. 'They were calling me curly-locks.'

Maria ruffled the silken curls lovingly. 'Take no notice, son. They are jealous because you are not like they are. They will never be more than peasants, while you . . . !' She gazed at him fondly. 'Who knows what you will be, François?' she said softly. 'Who knows?'

His father saw the matter differently. 'You stood up to them, eh?' He stood by the sink, drying his hands. 'Good for you, boy!' But there was something of surprise in his voice and the way his eyes narrowed as he stared searchingly at his changeling son. 'I wouldn't have expected it.'

'I can fight,' François said, his voice surly. 'I often have to.'

'Do you?' Both parents turned to look at him. His mother put out a hand towards him. 'Oh, son, you shouldn't!' She meant, *don't let them damage you, don't let them break your nose or scar your face.*

But his father was pleased. He stood for a moment, then grunted and turned away to eat his evening meal. François shrugged and climbed the narrow stairs to his bedroom. There, at least, he felt safe from everyone, parents and enemies alike.

The day was approaching, all too rapidly, when the boy's future would have to be decided. His father had never taken any notice of Maria's longings for her son's success; women were full of fancies—it was about the only thing you could say about them with any certainty. He would go into the fields with the other boys, the nonsense would be over once and for all, and the delicious dreams of his mother would fade like the pressed flowers from her marriage posy. Maria was beginning to grow desperate.

She was paying her weekly visit to the city market, walking through the streets in the centre of the town, when the great idea came to her. Here, away from the peasants haggling over the price of beans and the value of a pig, were the elegant places where the smart people could be found, the kind of people she hankered after in her own heart—the kind her husband only sneered at, without understanding the grace and dignity with which they passed through life. These were the kind of people for her François.

At a large plate-glass window Maria paused, regarding her reflection with displeasure. There was a pink ruffled curtain hiding the window from whatever lay within, and an overdressed Marie Antoinette wig proclaimed that this was a coiffeur's establishment. *'Maison Henri'* was written in gold letters, delightfully curlicued, over the shop front.

Maria stood deep in thought. As she did so a flicker of movement caught her eye and she turned to watch an elegant young man in impeccable clothes leading an elderly lady to the door and out to where a chauffeur waited by the kerb.

'A bientôt, Madame,' murmured the young man, bending over the fat hand proffered to him.

'Superlative, Henri!' gushed the old woman, using her eyes as she must have done when she was fifty years younger—before the folds of fat obscured their beauty. *'Formidable!'*

Maria watched her climb heavily into the car, lean forward to wave roguishly at Monsieur Henri, then back as the car gathered speed and drew away. At the door the young man stood, tall, slim and enchanting to her eyes, and the expression on his face was subtly changed as his client disappeared in the traffic.

'Fat fool!' he muttered viciously, and went back into the salon.

'To have such power!' Maria was saying to herself as she made her way back to the market. 'To have such wealthy women at one's mercy—to create beauty out of plainness, to have money, to move in such society. Oh!' She clasped her hands in emotional anguish, startling an ancient, dried-up nanny goat. 'Oh, this is what my François must have—this power. This wealth! He must be a hairdresser . . . '

It was a battle. Her husband first flatly refused to discuss the subject; then he grew very angry and said things she would never forget; and then he went out and got very drunk. François, sitting by the kitchen table while she sliced vegetables, stared at her face as she enumerated the advantages of life in the world of coiffure. He saw in her wildly enthusiastic expression some passion unknown among his companions; this was no crude longing, to be laughed at and demolished by cruel sarcasm. He thought about it for a long while that night, lying in bed under the rafters; and by the morning he had decided for himself that there was more future in coiffing the wealthy than in tilling his father's inhospitable land.

The battle was not over, but Maria's husband could recognise when he had lost the war. Skirmishing continued for weeks, but François and his mother showed a united front. When school closed on François for the last time it had all been arranged. On Monday morning he cycled into the town to present himself to Monsieur Henri—who took one look at the boy's boots and workaday clothes and deeply regretted having accepted responsibility for his training.

But within weeks he was congratulating himself on having seen the true ability in the boy's neat, quick hands, and the creativity hidden in that slim, curl-topped head. An advance of money had produced passable clothes; expert cutting had reduced the curly mop to elegant proportions. The boy had charm and he had instinctive good manners.

'Where did you learn such manners?'

'My mother,' said the boy without embarrassment. 'She had it in her mind from my birth that such things were important.'

His career thereafter, while not meteoric, was highly satisfactory. From Monsieur Henri he went to 'La Boutique', fifty miles from home; from there to 'Madeleine' on the outskirts of Paris. Maria sometimes felt that life was so good that she would almost be willing to die—if only she could be sure that one of the saints would keep her posted about François' triumphant march to the capital. Nothing could hold him back—and no amount of laughter could hurt him. François was a big man now.

But François, always outwardly calm in the face of his tormenting friends and relatives, had a deep central pool of hate within him, into which he fed every sneer, every comment, every pointed finger. It was a thing about him that no one could have guessed, for he seldom lost his temper, and in these days he managed to avoid the bloody nose and the black eyes, too. He went home once a year, carefully saving his holidays so that he could do what he knew his mother wanted—show himself off to the cackling dullards in the village.

This year was very important to him. After the holiday he would go back to Paris to open his own salon, in the smart area where film actresses and the wives of racing drivers could be seen. Among his clients would be a princess and several countesses, besides the current star of the opera. And so this would be the last visit home for François; after this year he would send for his mother to stay with him for a fortnight in the late summer (his father's death had made this possible), and the dusty cobbles of the village, the oily river, the country policeman looking for poachers, the grimy, garlic-impregnated inn would see his slim elegance no more. So it must be a year to remember.

'Go down to the inn,' his mother urged when he had eaten a huge country meal. 'They'll be so pleased to see you. Oh, son,' she whispered, fingering his midnight blue jacket and the creamy silk shirt sheer enough to reflect the colour of his skin through it, 'son, how proud I am of you!'

François pulled his jacket down resolutely, kissed her on her wrinkling cheek, and strode out manfully. It was not that he was scared—no one had tried to touch him for years—but the ribbing, the rudeness, the ribald comments were ineffably boring, the round, red faces doubly so.

Pierre was the first to see him; Pierre was an old school chum, now sporting a gigantic beer belly and a draggled bandit moustache.

121

'Well, it's the mother's son himself! Come here, François, old friend of my youth, and I'll buy you a beer.'

'That's a lovely piece of cloth,' said Martin, fingering the velvet jacket with his thick, grubby hands. 'Straight from a lady's boudoir!'

'And the hair,' said Bertrand, sniggering wetly into his drink. 'Could you make my hair go like that, François, my pet?' His eyes were running with tears of laughter as he pointed to his own bald pate. 'Oh, Monsieur François, I washed my hair and I can't do a thing with it!'

The noise was intolerable, the smell hideous. François was silent, drinking his drink, watching, saying nothing because he no longer knew their language. But his eyes were everywhere.

'We're here every day at this time,' Pierre cried, his eyes pink with merriment as François rose to leave them. 'Join us, my boy. We'll make a man of you yet!'

François heard the yells of laughter as he made his way down the road to his mother's house. He was very thoughtful. It *had* to be a year to remember.

Maria saw little of her son during the middle of each day. He arranged to have his main meal in the evening and took out with him a packet of sandwiches.

'Where do you go?' she asked, puzzled.

'Oh, around,' he said vaguely, kissing her cheek as he went to the door. 'To the inn for a drink first, then—who knows?'

Pierre and his friends had never enjoyed themselves so much. It beat cock-fighting altogether. Michel and Philippe had joined the gang, and the five men spent a happy half-hour baiting this new and sophisticated bear. 'He must break soon,' they murmured to each other, savouring the thought. 'This pansy creature cannot hold out for ever.'

But François had steel control. Two drinks and then he said farewell, very politely, and was gone. And when the summer drew to an end he left the village, never to return.

It was a clear autumn day when Pierre ran gasping into the inn and called for drinks all round. 'I'm to be a father,' he said in wonder when he could speak. 'My Jeannine is expecting a child! I'm to be a father!'

Martin's news came a week later. 'After so many years!' He wept happily into his beer. 'My little Juliet! I tell you—this winter she will not chop wood for the stove. I, Martin Leblanc, will do it!'

Bertrand's wife was forty-five if she was a day, and their children had been grown up and married for many a year when he, puzzled and lowering, broke the news to his friends.

'Another child! It's all very well, but a man wants his peace at my time of life. I shall still be working my fingers to the bone when I'm eighty at this rate.'

Michel slapped him on the back. 'There's life in the old dog! If you felt like that you should have kept away from her.'

Bertrand opened his mouth to say something, then closed it again. No one noticed because Philippe had just entered, his face sourly suspicious. 'Enough is enough! What's the matter with this place? Is there something wrong with the drains?'

The four men turned to look at him, slowly, as if they feared to hear his explanation. 'Your wife?' Pierre said at last.

'There's something very strange here,' Philippe muttered. 'What have they been up to?' They all turned to Michel, and he, stammering, turned red.

'Carole?' he whispered. 'Shall I see if she, too . . . ?' The men nodded and he stood unwillingly and went to the door.

The five women spent a contented winter visiting each other in their homes, cat-like in their contentment, never quite meeting each other's eyes. The men, suspicious of they knew not what, watched them with dark, lowering brows, and could discover nothing. In due time the village population was increased by four minuscule boys and one tiny girl. It was a spring harvest of seed sown in summer delight.

In the months that followed the happy fathers met in silent comradeship for their lunchtime beers. They spoke little of the children, not much of their wives.

'Tell me,' one would say suddenly, as if the words burst from him, 'does your wife . . . ?' and then he would stop. For the sons of the earth are not great and romantic lovers like the hairdressers of Paris, and it is difficult to know where one's wife could have learnt the little tricks of seduction and allurement that belong more properly to smart ladies who stroll on the boulevards in the morning sun.

There are things it is difficult to prove, and perhaps uncertainty is better than having one's suspicions bandied about in public. It is quite bad enough to have been deceived without having to admit that one was deceived by such a man—a fop, a pansy, a dummy draped in velvet! How could it be possible . . . ? The hardest to bear would be that cruel peasant laughter that respects no man.

So they met together in silence and departed to their homes a good two hours earlier than they had been used to doing. And Jeannine, Juliet, Charlotte, Lisa and Carole met to compare notes on their babies' progress, and never commented on the silken, curly hair or the fine, delicate features of their children.

And François was very busy that year, running his new salon. So he hardly ever wondered how things were going, in an obscure little village very far from Paris.

TIME TEST

It's hard to let go when age begins to demonstrate its limitations; but ultimately we all have to come to terms with it. Old Frank felt his life slipping away, out of his control; you can fight back, or you can back out gracefully. Either way has its difficulties. What would you have done?

TIME TEST

'What price experience?' Frank was muttering to himself. 'What price wisdom?' His hands (as always) were grimed with grease, his face too, from wiping away sweat. He stood up, straightened his back; there might be younger men with more sophisticated equipment, but he *knew* this locomotive, knew it like a father, a mother, a lover, all its quirks, all its meannesses, its moments of glory.

If they thought they could put him out to grass, they'd better think again. And then again! There wouldn't have been a locomotive at all but for him. *They* would have scrapped it, left it standing out in its paddock, a home for redback spiders and lizards and the odd long brown snake. No paint on it when he found it; no grease on the complaining axles, no power in the controlling levers. They had him to thank for its green and golden-brass perfection, its red-shiny wheels. Out to grass? Like someone had once done to his loco? No way!

'Look, Pops,' they had said, their eyes not meeting his, 'it's just one of those things. It comes to us all. You're entitled to a break—you've worked hard all your life . . . '

'And I'll go on working,' he had said, wielding the oilcan with threatening abandon so that they had stepped back, not quite sure of him. 'I'll work till I can't pull a lever or climb into the cab. And I don't see who's going to stop me!' He kept his back to them. The voice sounded strong, even belligerent; but he wasn't sure he could keep the fear out of his eyes.

127

Colin and young Frank looked at each other. 'Look, Dad,' Colin said, his hands clenched out of sight in his pockets. 'Look, Dad!'

'Look, Pops,' said young Frank nervously. 'You know . . . '

'I don't know nothing,' old Frank said, wiping his hands on a rag and turning away. 'Except that you're talking a lot of garbage. Experience is what counts. Experience! You don't get experience except by *doing* it. And I've done it.'

Colin and young Frank stared helplessly at each other. Once, perhaps, they could have taken it to a higher authority: Grandma, old Frank's missus, who could have graced the exalted ranks of the United Nations with her steel-framed, velvet-draped diplomacy. But Grandma was gone; and this was part of the trouble with the old man. One by one the things that mattered were being peeled away from him—health, strength, memory and his good companion of fifty years; what was left must be clung to.

An uncomfortable silence hung around old Frank until tea-time. No one was game to break into it, and he was too deep inside himself to be conscious of it. But sitting together around the family table demanded some kind of communication, and Colin passed a comment with the bread rolls.

'School holidays in a week.' No one answered. Everyone knew what he meant. The locomotive must be ready for the public, as it had been for years, squeak-free and rarin' to go.

'It'll be done,' old Frank said, tearing the roll in half and spreading marge on it as if it was on special.

'Yeah, I'm sure it will. But, you know, Dad . . . '

Merle, Colin's wife, lifted the cover on the vegie dish, and as the steam cleared she piled carrots and pumpkin on her husband's plate. 'Not now, you dumb-cluck!' she whispered to him. '*After!*'

Settled on the veranda, a stubby in his hand and another on the floor at his feet, old Frank waited for the next attack.

'*Now!*' Merle said softly, and escaped to the washing-up.

Probably they all meant to keep it low-key and reasonable. But where so many deep sentiments were involved it was bound to get out of hand.

'For cryin' out loud, Dad!' Colin shouted, when yet another impasse had been reached. 'Do you think you can go on forever?'

'No, I don't!' old Frank retorted. 'But it's not time yet. *No one* knows that loco like I do. I know every rivet, every nut and bolt. Who else knows it like me?'

'No one—*no one!* And why? Because no one's allowed near it. Great balls of fire—do you want to be *buried* in it?'

Young Frank watched the two men. He could feel the pain in his grandfather, but he could understand his father's sense of defeat, frustration.

'Look,' Colin said, pointing his finger at his father's chest. 'I want young Frank to take over the loco. Understand? It's time you gave him the chance. How's he going to learn?'

'Young Frank?' The old fellow turned and stared at the youth 'Let young Frank run my engine? He'd never do it! It'd be out of oil in a week. He's no mechanic. He hasn't had the training.' He gave a short, angry laugh.

The boy put a hand on his grandfather's arm. 'You could tell me. You could *show* me.'

'You gotta be born knowing,' the old man said, but he gave a sigh. 'You gotta have the feel in your hands.'

They left him to sit alone, out in the moonlight, and he could hear them inside the house, wrangling and snarling; and he laughed again, grimly, because he wasn't finished yet.

From where he sat he could see the fairground laid out in black and silver moonshine below him. His father had started it with a carousel and a shooting gallery, and he had expanded it, building with his own hands whatever he could not buy ready-made. When Colin was a youngster just out of school he had made him a partner; and the day Merle brought young Frank home from the hospital he had seen, in a kind of vision, a long line of Franks and Colins stretching away into eternity, each generation enhancing the work of its predecessor. It had never been a source of wealth; but it had filled a corner of his soul and given him a beacon to follow.

The locomotive had been his own final touch; he had found it by accident and renovated it with love. He had not minded handing the fairground over to his son; it made sense to let someone else do the worrying and balance the books. But he thought they might have let him keep his loco.

In the height of summer it would carry thirty at a time around the outer paddock, where kangaroos grazed and green parrots shot like arrows across the sun; and he, sitting on the engine, would dream as they chugged away from the noise of the sideshows, into the brief peace of the countryside and then back to the final straight and the little station he had built and painted when everyone said he was wasting his time.

He was up by six the next morning, silent, introspective, and out to the loco shed before anyone else was stirring. His hands worked as his mind wandered fancy-free—in the past, often; in the present, now and again. But never in the future. The future was a blank.

They would have to bring in another man soon, his mind suddenly and treacherously told him. It was too much for two men and a—and a what? A geriatric? He was darned if he was! You'd think they were in league to hurt him, to make him feel useless.

'He's afraid,' Merle said to Colin. 'He can see himself with nothing to do, nowhere to go.'

'That's stupid! He's got money put by. He could visit Aunt Kate. Go for a holiday.'

'On his own? Why would he want to?'

'Well, he's not running the blasted train! That's all! I'll give him something else to do. Sell tickets at the door—he could do that.'

'*I* do that,' Merle said patiently.

'Feed the birds in the aviary, then.'

'He doesn't like handling birds.'

'Sit on the veranda, then,' Colin said between his teeth, 'which is where the old fool ought to be at his age.' He stared morosely out of the window, down to the loco shed.

'What are you worried about?' Merle said over the teapot.

Colin turned away from the window. 'His age! If there was an accident, people would say it was because there was an old buffer driving it.'

'There's never been an accident.'

'So? Besides, *it's time*! Young Frank ought to be doing it. And the old boy ought to realise and stand down.'

The week passed slowly in a series of emotional fits and starts like a poorly-maintained motor. Paintwork, newly renovated, dried in the warming sun; the smell of engine oil and detergent filled the air. Old Frank kept to his shed; and when they met at mealtimes the three generations of men were stilted and easily offended.

'It's ridiculous!' Colin said on the Thursday. 'He's got to give in. You can't have a man of over eighty in charge of a locomotive. It's madness! It's probably illegal.'

He strode down to the shed, disturbing his father's meditations. He had been sitting on an old bench, gazing at the shining beauty before him, eating it up with his eyes, loving it with careful, stroking fingers. When Colin's arrival darkened the doorway he glanced up, his face closing.

'We gotta talk,' Colin said. 'At least, *I'm* going to talk, and you're going to listen.' He pulled a box forward and sat down. His father, surprisingly, did not try to interrupt.

He put all the arguments, cogently, purposefully: age, infirmity, danger of accident. He offered him a choice of aviary, tickets or veranda. He suggested a holiday in Bali, on the Barrier Reef—anywhere! Finally, he gave a nervous laugh, for the old boy's continued silence was disconcerting, uncomfortable.

'Besides, Dad, you may *think* you've got the old loco properly under control—but you're slowing down, you know. You've been taking a full minute longer than you used to for the round trip. And time's money in this game. You know that.'

Old Frank narrowed his eyes. All his good resolutions sickened and died. 'Slower?' he said. 'Since when, slower? You been timing me?'

131

'Last holidays,' Colin said nervously. He thought it had been going too well. 'Just a couple of times.'

'Bloody cheek!' Old Frank snorted. 'Young pip-squeak! Think I can't keep speed up? I'll show you!' He stood up, forgetting his age, his good intentions. 'All right—time me! Get out your stop-watch and *time me!*' He stumped angrily out into the sunlight. 'Better than that—send young Frank round first, since you seem to fancy him on the loco. Let young Frank do it—*and then see me beat him!*'

Colin watched him go up the track to the house, heard the screen door bang first, then the back door; could imagine Merle's face. He sighed. 'You gotta admire the old coot,' he said to the locomotive, and kicked its immaculate wheel.

The time trials were set for Friday morning. Old Frank wouldn't be budged from his challenge. Young Frank took the whole thing as a bit of a joke to begin with; but by mid-morning he was tense, sensing that somehow he had become a pawn in the power struggle between father and son. Besides, he was afraid he might not be able to outshine the old boy. He hadn't often been allowed to drive the precious engine.

'Of course you can do it,' his father said shortly. 'Don't take it too fast on the curves. But go like the clappers on the straight. And do it quicker than he can. *Please?*' They stared at each other.

'I'll try.'

'Don't bother *trying*. Do it!'

'You go first, Pops,' the boy said politely.

Old Frank snorted. 'No fear! You go—and then *I'll beat your time!* Whatever it is.'

Merle looked uneasy. 'He'll kill himself.'

'Don't talk rot.' Colin took out his stopwatch 'Right, young Frank!'

Frank sat himself on the driver's seat, staring ahead of him over the miniature smoke-stack, seeing the parallel lines of the track drawing together until they appeared to become one and disappeared round the first bend. He swallowed.

'Ready?' Colin shouted. The locomotive seemed to be trembling with expectancy. '*Now!*' Frank pulled the levers, the wheels gripped the track, and he was off.

The clatter and beat entered his body, the wind pulled at his hair as he sped around the bend and entered the stretch where a mini-town had been built The castle, the row of country cottages, the duck-pond all shot past him; and he felt the exhilaration, knew a sense of belonging as his hands rested on the controls, had a moment of kinship with the rhythmic pounding of his grandfather's locomotive.

Another bend, then into the paddock. 'Go, you beauty!' he cried, his voice whipped away over the trees by the speed of his passing.

The final curve showed him the last straight and the station; his father was standing, watch in hand, and his grandfather, his face tight and expressionless.

'Five minutes, thirty-seven seconds,' Colin said, holding himself in. But young Frank could see the triumph in his eyes. 'A full minute-and-a-half off your time, Dad.'

'Without passengers,' growled the old man. 'What d'you think I am? A fool? They'd have fallen off at the bends.' He glared at young Frank. 'I suppose you think you're a real fine fellow?'

'No, Pops.' He grinned suddenly. 'But I liked the feel of it.' The old man grunted.

'Your turn, Dad.' Colin reset the watch. For a moment old Frank simply stood and stared at the loco. He rubbed a dusty spot with his finger, then, stiffly but with the rhythm of long practice, climbed on to the seat. He took his peaked cap from his pocket, pulled it down over his eyes, nodded to his son, his face grim with concentration.

'Ready?' Colin said. 'Then—*go!*'

The train began to move. It chugged for a few seconds and then gathered speed. Anxiously they watched it out of sight.

Old Frank let his hands caress those brass levers. The train was fairly spanking along, and here, away from his son's accusing eyes, he could ignore the animosity and experience again the fascination of a perfectly-maintained piece of machinery doing its job superbly.

He forgot about time. He talked to the locomotive: 'Just a little more, a little more . . . and then slowly, slo-owly round the bend . . . ' He nodded to the midget ducks on the miniature duck-pond, waved to the figure fixed forever by a cottage gate, at the face showing palely at a window of the castle. 'Good-day to you—howya going'?' And on, on into the paddock: 'How's tricks today, Skippy?'

Impulsively he took off his cap, threw it far from him.

They flew round the last bend, the carriages bouncing heartily behind him. The wind (or something) had brought tears into his eyes, but he didn't try to hide them. Colin was there, his gaze not on the watch but on his father as the train drew to a perfectly timed halt. Young Frank was smiling cheerfully; Merle had joined them. She came to him and gave him a hand to dismount. Old Frank laid a gentle touch on the engine and then turned away.

'Well,' Colin said, a little breathless, as if he had run with them, 'there you go! I wouldn't have believed it.'

'Believed what?' the old man said.

'Five minutes—thirty-*one* seconds! You beat your grandson. Congratulations!'

For a moment, a long moment, they stared at each other, father and son, antagonists; and then old Frank nodded and wiped his forehead.

'But . . . ' young Frank said, and his father hushed him with a raised finger.

'Calls for a beer, Merle,' Colin said. 'Come on, old feller—back to the house.'

'Dad,' said young Frank in a low voice, but urgently, 'Dad, why did you say Pops had won?'

Colin looked at his son, almost ashamed. 'I couldn't do it to him, Frank. At the end I couldn't tell him he was nearly a minute slower. I'm sorry.'

'So we're back to square one?'

'Well—yes. But it can only be a matter of time. He can't go on forever—can he?' They exchanged comically wry glances.

After lunch old Frank stumped along the narrow track to the loco shed. He removed the padlock and entered the warm, gloomy interior, redolent with the odours of paint and grease and polish—good smells, wholesome smells that summed up a man's working life.

He regarded the locomotive. The brass fittings shone with the strength of his own muscles and repeated applications of polish. Would anyone else care as he had?

Colin and young Frank were testing the carousel when he joined them; Colin turned off the noisy engine and the two men faced each other.

'No one's going to take her from me, you know, Col,' old Frank said after an uncomfortable pause.

'I know, Dad.'

'It's my loco.'

'Of course it is.'

'But I can *give* it, can't I?' He turned to his grandson and held out a key. 'Here you are, young Frank. Mind you treat her good.'

He turned away in the sudden silence, then looked back at Colin. 'I've got a watch, too, you know. I can tell the difference between five and six minutes!' He snorted. 'You must think I'm a galah. Senile, eh? Five minutes and thirty-one seconds! Hah!' They watched him go.

When he opened the back door, took a deep breath after the short climb, Merle was in the kitchen.

'Where d'you keep the bird-seed?' he said, and winked at her.

NOTHING LIKE A FAMILY

This is a different kettle of fish! It was written as an entry for a monologues competition in 2009—it didn't win. It all takes place in 'Mum's' kitchen, and was intended to be acted by one woman, talking to you—that is, the audience. We never know her name, and her way of dealing with life might not appeal to us, but those of us with families can appreciate the loyalty, even while we deplore the lifestyle.

NOTHING LIKE A FAMILY

*S*he comes in, clearly exhausted. She is mid-forties, tough, but a little defeated by the problems of life. She sits down in the only comfortable chair and gives a great sigh. She has a big shopping bag, which she puts down carefully beside her. She is holding a mug of tea which she sips from time to time. She slips her shoes off, clearly relieved, and wriggles her toes.

She has been 'Mum' and 'the old girl' for so long that it is pointless to give her a personal name.

(*Fanning herself*) Crikey, it's hot, I'n'it? All I could think about over there was a cup of tea. All the time Georgie was talking—what was it he wanted? (*Looks around vaguely*) I wrote it down somewhere—oh—never mind, it'll do later . . .

Georgie—he was a lovely baby, Georgie was. Well, they was all lovely babies in their own way, I s'pose. But Georgie had those lovely blue eyes—an' dark hair—an' he'd look up at you and grin . . . Best o' the bunch, Georgie was.

You have hopes for them, don't you? You think, *this* time we'll do it right. But they get to 14—15—and what can you do? Minds of their own at 14. Well, Georgie had a mind of his own at 7. He'd look at you with those big blue eyes, and what could you do?

I s'pose it all started for Georgie when he stole that thing from the hardware an' I didn't make him give it back. I was going to—but he looked at me and grinned . . . though what he wanted

137

with that great spanner thing I'm sure I don't know. No use to a kid, a thing like that. It was just bad luck that school kid came round the next day. Not a very nice kid. Bit of a bully, I think. Badly brought up. Bigger than Georgie. Next thing, that kid's on the ground and Georgie's holding the spanner.

(*Like a sigh*) . . . Yeah . . .

I said to him, I said, 'You shouldn't ought to have done that, Georgie. But it was an accident, Georgie said—an' you've got to believe your kids, haven't you?

We've just got the two of them, Wayne and Georgie. There was a little girl, too. Sophie. Pretty little thing. Had one o' them mysterious cot deaths. Right as rain one minute, then—gone! Wayne was ten, supposed to be looking after her. He comes running out to me where I'm hanging out the nappies. 'Not breathing,' he said. 'She's not breathing.' And she wasn't. She wasn't breathing . . .

Yeah . . .

They came, police an' all—but there wasn't any real evidence. Wayne said he was sorry—and you've gotta believe them.

Wayne was always a bit of a lad. Mis*chee*vious! But he managed to stay out of trouble—with the cops, that is. Not with his dad. Dreadful hard on him, his dad was. Hand of iron! Reckon that was why he got caught. Well, kids need a bit o' fun now and then, don't they?

And here he was up this end of the street, and that toffee-nosed lot at the other end's having a party, aren't they? So young Wayne got his mates together and went to the party. Bit o' fun! Probably better if they'd had an invite but . . .

I didn't know he'd taken matches and a bottle o' petrol, did I? Mind you, I heard the noise when the palm tree went up. Quite a show it was. People shouldn't be allowed to let those frond things hang down. Asking for trouble.

Well, the cops got him for that. You'd 'a' thought for a first offence . . . but they said they'd had their eye on him. And once that lot gets the knife in you can say goodbye. I think it was because they'd taken that petrol. Premeditated, they said.

Course, his dad nearly killed him when he came home. Mad as a cut snake because Wayne had nicked *his* petrol. Huh! I wonder where *he* got it from in the first place. Course, it's not so easy now they've got locks on everything. It's a crying shame, I think, that people don't trust each other anymore.

But all that was years ago. I was real proud of Wayne when he got that job on the building site. 'You can make something of yourself,' I said. Course, he's a strong boy. Good muscles. He was going great before that silly business of the toilets. You'd have thought he'd've found a market for them first, wouldn't you? His dad said it just showed.

It wasn't only Wayne. There was his mate Stevie. Mind, I was never quite sure about Stevie. Funny family! They did everything together, those two boys, right from primary school. Everything! Truanted together. Used to go down to the river and swim—well, that's what they said they did. I wondered sometimes. They'd come home quite dry, no towels nor nothing. 'So what've you been doing?' I'd say, and they'd look at each other a bit funny and say 'Nothing'. 'Could have stayed in school, then,' I'd say. Stayed in school and done nothing! Yeah . . . Didn't seem to learn much, neither of them. Not schoolwork, anyway.

It was something about Stevie's eyes, I think. Made you wonder what was going on behind them. Not like Wayne. He'd stare you down even while he was lying—well, yes, he was a bit of a liar, I have to admit it. But his dad was so tough on him it wasn't worth telling the truth—he'd never believe him, not if he was to say he'd been to church. More likely to ask him what he'd nicked from the reverend! No—Wayne would stare straight at you and swear he was telling the truth even while they was putting the cuffs on him. But you've gotta believe them, haven't you—your own kids?

They was waiting for Wayne when he got to Brissy. I didn't know he'd ever been to Queensland. He never told *me*. A break-in, the cops said. But I reckon it was because of what happened to his dad.

Wayne reckoned he'd been set up. Some guy he knew. I'd believe that. Wayne's not really a bad boy. Just unlucky, really, that security man coming in just as he had his hands on a diamond bracelet. Wayne said the bloke wasn't supposed to be round that side of the building just then.

Anyway, he told them he was putting the thing back. Unlucky! He's always been a bit unlucky.

Like that business with the girl, what was her name? Daphne? Deirdre? No, Sylvia, that was it. Deirdre was the other one. You tell 'em to take care when they're—well, you know what boys are. It's all sex, isn't it, at that age? 'Don't bring home no babies,' I said. 'Not till you're old enough to look after them. Because I'm not going to . . . ' No! I done my bit for the kids. If they gets caught they can bloody well get themselves out of it. Then this girl comes round. Screaming and yelling she was. 'Your Wayne's got me pregnant and now he says he don't want it.'

Well, they don't, do they? Not at that age. What was he—eighteen? Too young to be a dad. I mean, look at his father—he was twenty when we—well, when Wayne got started. Disaster! I thought my mum'd kill him. My dad nearly did. But the police could see it was just a domestic. They didn't take much notice of domestics in them days.

So somewhere we've got a little bastard. I told her to get rid of it. But her folks are religious—not very practical. They moved away. Just as well, really. Wayne never talks about it. Well, I reckon he never thinks about it. Put it out of his mind—probably the best in the end.

I was thinking about it the other day. It'd be about eight now, I suppose. Don't know if it's a boy or a girl. And then I suddenly thought—that's my grandchild. Never really thought about it before. My grandchild—yeah . . .

Wayne learnt *his* lesson. Leastways, I suppose so. There hasn't been any more young ladies screaming round! Hasn't got a girl, not at the moment. Seems to go through them at a rate o' knots, does Wayne. Never seems to be the same one twice. And Georgie . . . well, I don't know about Georgie. He's so good-looking you'd think the girls'd be round like bees round honey. He's got very friendly with Stevie—you know, Wayne's friend. He's that bit older, of course. They go fishing together—last year they went camping—you can bet your bottom dollar that when Georgie gets out Stevie'll be there at the gates. I've wondered sometimes . . . but I try not to think about it. If they was, you know, *special* friends, I wouldn't answer for his dad's reaction. *Poofters*, he'd say. It's not a very nice word. Still, be thankful for small mercies! At least he wouldn't be getting a girl in the family way.

Well, I suppose I'd better get along and see my old man. He likes me to drop in of an afternoon. I take a few things he likes . . . just little things. (*Takes out a bottle of whisky and a pack of cigarettes*). Says it makes the day go quicker. He's not one for lying about in hospitals. But you can't do much with two broken legs and a plate in your face, can you? Young Wayne was really angry that time . . . yeah . . .

But I told him. 'They're both bigger than you are now, mate,' I said. 'Time'll come when they won't take it anymore.'

But they don't listen, do they? Everything the hard way. Never learn. I can still see the look on his face when Wayne went for him! Yeah . . .

They've put a plate in. I don't know what they mean, really—putting a plate in his face. I mean—it was a plate what done it in the first place. Wayne, throwing it at his dad. 'Wayne,' I said. 'Wayne, that's naughty!' He's got a really good eye, young Wayne. If Georgie had thrown it, it probably wouldn't have done the same amount of damage. But they think the eye's going to be OK. I always reckoned Wayne could probably be a test cricketer if he'd put his mind to it. Very straight thrower.

I shan't be visiting Wayne. Well, Brisbane's a long way, isn't it? And he'll be out in eight months. Time flies, don't it? Well, it's what they say—time flies when you're having fun!

Oh, well!—I suppose they'll all be home again one day. Like the old days, it'll be.

Nothing like a family, is there?

THE REUNION

The Bicentenary celebrations of a couple of decades ago—can it really be that long?—brought people together from all over the place. But every street party, every joyful activity had to have a motivating personality prepared to go without sleep to achieve the almost impossible. Harriet's passion to make her party an event to remember led her to a place she had never expected.

This story was 'commended' the following year in the Coolum and Inter-state Writers Association competition.

142

THE REUNION

Harriet stared out of the window across the rooftops of her suburb to the sparkle of light delineating the river. She had done too much staring lately; nearly two years of it, her eyes on the distance, her mind somewhere else. Sometimes she caught Tom's gaze on her, thoughtful, patient, ready to help when he knew what the problem was. Thank God for Tom!

Everyone would look back on the bicentenary, she told herself; everyone would have a different perspective, satisfaction or disappointment or simply thankfulness that it was all over. But not everyone, surely, would enter this third century aware of having found something very precious—and then lost it forever?

Would she have taken on her self-imposed task if she had known the outcome? That was the teaser. She thought she knew the answer now; in spite of her sense of emptiness, Harriet acknowledged that the experience had been so rare that, even if she had known, she could not have avoided it.

Everything starts somewhere, of course; this undertaking had begun with a letter to the papers. She would have called it back, if she could, the moment she saw it there, with her own name at the bottom, Harriet Weston. But by then it was too late.

The concept came out of the blue. Someone at the cricket club dance said, 'I reckon all our skeletons will be out of their closets by 1988,' and she had laughed. There were plenty of bicentennial schemes starting to float, but she saw nothing for her in them.

'What do you mean?'

'Everyone's fossicking back, trying to find someone who came out to Botany Bay. It's the new aristocracy.'

She smiled. 'My closets are empty. No skeletons! No scandals—just dull, good-living country people. Sorry!'

'How boring!' someone said, and they changed the subject.

But Harriet was caught by a frisson of excitement, and it would not leave her, lying dormant for days and then suddenly popping up when she least expected it. Who *were* her forebears? Where had they lived, and how? Where were their roots, in those old northern hemisphere countries? And, ultimately, who was she, the descendant of so many who, stringing back through time, carried her to the threshold of Creation itself? She had never thought like this before, never seen herself mirrored endlessly into the oblivion of the ages; and she sat now, in her leisured moments, and wondered.

In the library her appetite was further stimulated. 'I want to trace my ancestors,' she said, feeling foolish; but the librarian knew all about such requests, and Harriet sat behind a pile of books and tried to pretend she was no stranger to research.

And so—the letter! Perhaps there were other members of the family who could add fact to her fantasy? She knew her grandmother had had two brothers, her grandfather a sister. But where were they, where were *their* offspring? Australia is an easy place for losing contact.

'I am planning a reunion of the families of John George Barton and Edwina Carstairs, who were married on September 13th, 1890, at Crombie Heights, Western Australia. Will all interested people please contact . . . ?'

'No one will answer,' she told herself, cutting out the slip of paper and placing it carefully in the scrap-book she had decided to keep in spite of her pessimism.

But they did! The first was a tentative phone-call from an elderly distant cousin who had lived for the past twenty years only four streets away. She recalled Aunt Edwina and Uncle John, and had met Edwina's mother, Harriet's great-grandmother, just once in the years before the Great War. Harriet began to make a family tree on a large sheet of graph paper. She was hooked; husband Tom found that his comfortable lifestyle was under siege before the urgent pressure of Harriet's passionate enthusiasm.

Others came to the surface throughout the city, rising like bubbles from the bottom of a pond. Then a country cousin remembered stories from the days of Queen Victoria, and another had a comprehensive photograph album which, because it was too precious to be allowed out of the house, took Harriet away from home for a night.

It was all-pervasive. She awoke in the mornings with her dreams resolving, mist-wise, into the actuality of these long-gone people who, in some strange and almost mystical way, were a part of her. Her kitchen, her neat, old-fashioned house and the herb garden perfuming the summer air were, for the first time, not enough. She lived now with shadows, with formless figures and featureless faces, striving to clothe them with flesh, to fill out their outlines, discover their personalities, reconstruct their lives and loves.

'Don't you think this is getting out of hand?' Tom said quite mildly, indicating the books, the piles of notes, the sepia photographs that had invaded the peace of his sitting room. 'Where will it all lead?'

She gazed at him earnestly. 'We have a duty to them! We ought to know where we've come from—who we are.'

'I know who I am,' he retorted, disgruntled. 'And I used to know who you were!'

'Be patient,' she pleaded. 'I have to go on. I have to find out! I've got back to 1850—don't stop me, Tom.'

He shrugged, good-natured, easy-going; and Harriet quelled her momentary unease and buried herself in photo-copied lists of names and places.

Her research showed her that her grandmother's family had arrived in Australia in 1869, and she was able to locate many descendants on that side of the family, calling a halt shen she arrived at the names of James Carstairs and his wife Sarah, who had emigrated as servants to New South Wales, and led dull, exemplary lives.

What she wanted was to find someone more dynamic, more exciting, more—*romantic*, she admitted to herself. A figure she could clothe with mystery, someone who would be her very own, loosened from the bonds of death and the tyranny of time; an Adam, created new out of the heartaches and tragedies of his era, standing strong and commanding across the twilight of history.

She intensified her search into her father's family, approaching it from a different angle, going through the pages of names of teeming multitudes of petty criminals and social misfits who had been the country's first settlers, however unwillingly.

'Barton . . . Barton . . . Barton! But which one—how can I tell?' Then a stroke of luck here, an apocryphal tale there from a newly discovered relative, and a Christian name, a letter, an old, old photograph, and she knew!

'I've found him!' she called to Tom; and he, loving her, pretended he was interested. Harriet, unable to transmit to him her sense of wonder and excitement, felt frustration; but he patted her arm, nodded over her evidence, smiled reassuringly and with kindness. It had to suffice.

The reunion was a great success. Everyone said so. It took place over a long weekend, and they came from as far as New Zealand in order to be present. Harriet was enraptured. Nearly a hundred people cared enough to make the trip; and though she had never organised anything bigger than a cricket tea she found she was in her element.

On the Saturday evening she made the first speech of her life. They had hired the Anglican church hall, and as she looked around at the faces turned towards her she felt a great wave of affectionate warmth leave her to flow over these good folks who shared with her this one thing above all others—they were linked, one way or another, to that one man, the person she had pursued across two centuries, the man who had changed her life: Abel George Barton, transported convict, emancipist, farmer, merchant seaman and, at last, respected elder of the community, who had founded this great family of which she was a proud and happy member.

She told them about Abel. 'Raise, your glasses,' she said with a catch in her voice, 'and drink to all our progenitors—and to Abel George Barton!'

'*Abel George Barton . . .* ' she heard the name ricochet around the room and was content. Turning to Tom, she put her hand in his and leaned against his shoulder.

'Thank you,' she whispered. 'I had to get it out of my system.' He nodded, squeezed her hand; he knew her—he understood.

Sunday was warm and sunny. No day more perfect for a barbecue. The hundred or so relatives of Abel George milled cheerfully around fire-filled drums, enduring smoke and flies for the pleasure of each other's company and the delights of a well-turned steak and crisp salad. Harriet gazed about her with quiet satisfaction. The strange frenzy of the last months was over.

'You'll have to write a book!' someone said through a mouthful of coleslaw; she laughed and shook her head.

'Me? Never! I'm going back where I belong—I've been neglecting Tom.' And she really meant it.

Tom had brought camping chairs, and he leaned back and pulled his hat over his eyes, ready to sleep in the warm afternoon shade. Harriet cleared their plates away and repacked the picnic basket, before wandering among the trees, chatting to new-found friends. The atmosphere was already changing; there would be an exodus shortly, hotel bills to pay, planes to catch, and memories of this one strange moment in time when she had done something that now seemed to her immensely, tremendously meaningful.

There was a tree-trunk lying across a clearing, and a man sat on it, regarding the well-fed, somnolent throng. Somewhere a younger group spun Frisbees through the golden air, but here it was quiet, remote, utterly peaceful. She smiled at him and sat down.

'Your party has been a success.' His voice was deep and strong, but gentle too. She nodded.

'Yes, indeed. More than I could have expected.'

'And now you will all go your separate ways.' He paused. 'I would like to thank you, but . . . '

'Oh, please, it has been such a pleasure. I can't tell you. The one really exciting thing I have ever done in my life.'

He was smiling at her, and she blushed. 'You did it well.'

'Which side of the family . . . ?' She hesitated. He was a man of striking appearance, yet she did not remember having seen him all weekend.

'I'm a Barton.' He nodded. 'It's good to see so many descendants.'

'That's what I thought.' She turned to look at him, but the setting sun was behind his head and his face was almost dark, the greying hair an aura around it. 'What's your name?'

'Abel George.'

She sat for a moment, then laughed. 'I didn't know we still had an Abel George! Where are you from?'

'Oh, I've had to travel. It was a long way. But it was worth it—to see, to know.'

She found her voice with difficulty. 'To know what?'

'That one is not quite forgotten.'

There was a heavy pause. Much as she wanted to, Harriet dared not look into his eyes. The sun had slipped a little lower, and she felt his gaze on her.

'Are you saying . . . ?' she started, then stopped again. 'There are Bartons from New Zealand. Are you with them?'

'Harriet!' he said with laughter in his voice. 'You have chased me through the centuries! Don't you recognise me?'

Then she looked at him, and briefly the shadow lifted so that she saw him clear and bright as a summer dawn. She put out a hand to him, but he shook his head.

'We can't cross the barrier,' he murmured; and in that moment she yearned for something as she had never yearned before: the touch of his hand on hers, a sensation of his physical nearness. Some unexplored part of her mind knew that Abel George had changed her life forever. She turned to look through the trees to the

148

place where Tom sat, his hand now shielding his eyes, searching for her. When she turned back, the stranger was gone.

She wandered across the dry grass, nodding and smiling as she went, and sat down beside Tom. Within her was an empty sensation, the pain of loss, bringing her close to despair.

'I wondered where you'd gone,' her husband said.

'I was sitting on that tree trunk. See it? There was a man. We talked.'

'Yes, I saw you. But you were alone. I was watching.'

She smiled at him. 'You're right. I was imagining . . . '

'What did you imagine?'

For a while she did not speak. 'Abel George,' she said at last. 'I believe he enjoyed his party.' Tom glanced down at her, raising his eyebrows. She sighed. 'I think maybe I've fallen in love with him.'

Tom stretched and yawned as cars began to draw away along the track. 'I've known that for months.' He folded up his camping chair. 'Good luck to him!' He picked up the picnic basket.

Harriet drew in a deep breath of gum-scented, smoke-tinged air. For a moment so brief that she doubted her eyes she saw him again, Abel George, standing among the dusky trees; it seemed as if he raised his hand to her over a great distance, and then, leaving her eternally bereft, was gone.

NATIVITY

A reunion looks back to days gone by; nativity, whether it's the babe lying in a manger or our own lovely babes gurgling in their cribs, looks forward. And it's not surprising that we celebrate birth; each child that is born carries with it the hopes for the future, and even when we know that there are no guarantees we still hold on to that hope. But along with all the starry eyes of new parents (and the too-long nights during teething) there is always the nativity play. I hope that this particular tradition will never die.

This story appeared in The West Australian newspaper and the South African magazine, Fair Lady.

NATIVITY

I make no apology for bringing up the subject of nativity plays. If you've ever produced one, nothing I can say will surprise you; and if you haven't, you wouldn't believe me anyway.

I was absolutely determined that I wouldn't do it this year. People take things for granted. When you've done something twice it becomes part of the ritual. 'Oh, Jane does that,' they say. Good old Jane! No husband, no children; just two cats and a pet cocky in that neat little cottage in the old part of our tiny town. None of those excuses that other people make when they don't want to do something. Jane will do it!

'Besides,' they say cunningly, 'you do it so well. Always the same, and yet always something different. You have a Gift!'

I even lied. 'I may not be here for Christmas. I may be going away.' But no one listened. 'Go away afterwards,' they said, as if my personal life carried no weight.

So there I am in mid-October, trying to work out a new angle. It's not easy. The story must remain unviolated; innovations are frowned upon. But familiarity can breed boredom. The need to surprise is still there, even in a nativity play.

Real animals around the crib? May Cotter has a donkey. Daphne Bowen's old milk cow would probably stand still out of sheer weariness. But the wooden floor of the community hall's ageing platform would never bear the weight, and it's a bit much to expect small children to share the billing with animals that have, presumably, never been house-trained.

151

Modern dress? 'Making it relevant'? No way! This is the season for Tradition. Ignore it at your peril.

So—the mixture as before. Daphne makes a lovely Gabriel. She stands at the back of the stage, a gold-foil-covered book in hand, and narrates. Her husband, Jimmy, rigs up a spotlight that illuminates her like the fairy on the Christmas tree.

The vicar isn't at first sure about Daphne. He says Gabriel should be male. I say surely an archangel is sexless, a supernatural being not in need of classification. The vicar is a bit short with me, pointing out that Daphne, with seven children to her credit, is hardly sexless. I remind him that six of Daphne's seven are in the play, and he acknowledges my argument. This will be Daphne's fourth year as Gabriel, and I must say she does it with style.

Looking back, I think I may have sold myself a bit short. I am not a withered spinster, though I shall never see the right side of thirty again. The lack of a husband may well be remedied when John comes marching home; and one hopes (blushing demurely) that the production of offspring will follow at carefully regulated intervals thereafter.

Meanwhile, I run a little arty-crafty shop in the town and am known for my impeccable good taste. No, I mean it! Mrs Vicar was once heard to say, after a parish fete, that the handwork stall had been managed by Jane 'with her usual impeccable taste'.

It's a pity I can't run my life the same way. John would never have marched off in the first place if I hadn't put him through a series of ludicrous tests. I wanted to be sure; so many friends have married in rapture and divorced in pain. Our marriage was to be perfect. It was only when he said, his voice grating with frustration, that he felt like a monkey on a barrel organ, standing on his head to win applause, that I realised how amazingly stupid I was being. He marched away the next day, righteously affronted, and signed on for a year on an oil rig.

It took me six months, writing three times a week, to convince him that I had seen the error of my ways, and another three weeks to persuade him to pop the question again. 'Come home and ask me,' I begged. But he said he had taken a vow to stay away for a year and a day, and nothing would make him break it. Romantic fool!

So all the lines are converging for me towards the week before Christmas. The nativity play is well into rehearsal, and my approaching engagement (the real thing: proposal, ring and celebration) is rarely out of my mind. The shop is as busy as I've ever seen it, and I am at peace with the world.

Silly me! Herod and the Third Shepherd go down with chickenpox in early December. One of the Wise Men falls off his skateboard and is temporarily hospitalised, returning with a black eye which wins him great admiration from the Heavenly Host, who are this year's innovation, having learnt to sing 'Glory to God in the highest' to a tune composed by Merv, organist and master of five choristers.

But the show must go on. The Third Shepherd is no great loss, and easily replaced. Herod, with quite a demanding speaking part—three full sentences—is another matter. Auditions produce no one with the necessary qualities of aggression and nasal sneer that come naturally to young Wayne, son of the local publican. In the end the First Wise Man has to exchange wisdom for despotism, and can be seen muttering his new lines in the corner by the ancient boiler.

I promote one of the two remaining Magi, and appoint a rather small boy with a lisp to the position of Second Wise Man. 'Right!' I say in clear tones that reach to the back of the hall. 'No one is to be sick, or break a bone, or go to visit grandma, until the play is over.' I believe I have covered everything.

It isn't Joseph's fault that his father chooses the week before Christmas to run off with the girl from the petrol bowsers.

'You can understand,' says his mother, sniffing bravely, 'how he feels. He loves his dad. Now he says he won't stand up in front of everyone, knowing that *they know.*' She looks at me anxiously out of red eyes.

'But it might help him,' I say selfishly. Selfish, because how could it help? The child must be devastated. But where will I find another Joseph?

'Well, he won't do it.' She sniffs again and blows her nose and keeps on being brave, and I put my hand on her arm and, nearly as bravely, say of course we can manage, and is there anything I can do? I have a sudden vision of the petrol girl and wonder why any man in his right mind would think the world well lost for her. 'I don't think he's in his right mind,' Joseph's mother says, eerily echoing my thoughts. 'His dad, I mean. What's she got that I haven't got?'

I detach one of the Heavenly Host and tell him he'll have to be Joseph. It's only when I see him next to Mary that I realise that he's about half her size. Well . . . ! There's nothing in the Bible about Joseph's height relative to Mary's. *My* Mary will simply have to bend a bit.

The final week, and I am so busy in the shop that by the evening it's all I can do to feed the cats and tease Cocky, let alone get down to the hall and direct my thespian forces. Letters to John grow scrappy, and I can feel my reserves of energy lapping the bottom of the reservoir. 'Come home, John,' I moan into my mirror, viewing with distaste a large pink lump which, in the manner of such things, will become empimpled just in time for The Night.

Three nights to go, and the Innkeeper goes down with 'flu. We are out of participating boys now; entreaties to a couple of year 3 lads are met with a 'no *way*' that demolishes argument. The Innkeeper will have to be a girl, and the only girl available at this late date is, appropriately enough, the daughter of Greg and Annie who run our very small town's only motel. I have avoided young Belle up to now—an offensively knowledgeable child with a sideways look that scorns adults. On second thoughts, what better expression for rejecting two weary travellers.

One day to go, and dress rehearsal attended by the local kindies. In daylight, of course, which robs it of some charm and theatricality, but a reasonable success if you set your standards low enough. Daphne's youngest, Milly, bursts into tears when she locates her mother on the stage, and escapes her kindy teacher; so we let her sit at her mother's feet and pretend we can't see her.

154

Daphne's husband stays on afterwards to work on the lighting; and it is while I am making my after-supper-cuppa that a strange glow begins to light the trees standing between my little cottage and the hall. I gaze, afraid to think what it might mean; but within moments it is all too clear: the hall is on fire.

What a night! 'Early to bed,' I had told myself; 'you deserve it.' In fact, we are all out there in the moonlight, gazing in fascination at the wooden hall as it falls in on itself, here a rafter flaring up and then collapsing in sparkling pyrotechnics, there a window popping in the heat, strange writhings behind it as curtains shrivel and are consumed. It's three o'clock, with the moon watching dispassionately from above as we scurry, antlike, around the ruins, before we feel it is safe to leave.

I am suffering from acutely mixed feelings—all that preparation, to come to nothing. But somewhere underneath there is a growing bubble of relief. No nativity play! No one could expect it, now. 'What happened?' I ask Jimmy. 'Electrics!' he says curtly.

I have hardly fallen asleep when there is hammering on the door, and a man's voice saying, 'Get up, woman! Are you going to lie in bed all day?' John! John, home three days early! I fly to the door, and you will forgive me if I draw a veil over the next hour or so.

'Yes,' he says as we sit over breakfast, 'a vow is a vow. Shall I go away again?' I assure him that won't be necessary. 'I thought I'd get back in time for the play, since it's about the only thing you've mentioned in the past month.'

I tell him about our frantic, frenzied night. No, no one was hurt. No, all the children had their costumes at home. Yes, it was a pity. No, it couldn't be done. Where? There's nowhere else except the church, which is very tiny, and traditionally it has always been done in the hall, and . . .

'Out of doors,' John says firmly. 'Moonlight. On the oval. We'll fix some lighting . . . '

'But . . . '

'I'll go round to see Jimmy.'

'But ...'

'You get down to the shop. I'll fix something.

I regard him thoughtfully. A year away has done something to him. This is not the man I once put to the test. He's got it all together now, and I'll have to watch my step. I feel a tiny quiver of apprehension, followed by a rushing cataract of love. 'Yes, dear,' I say, and leave him the washing up.

The phone must have run hot all day. I let my little assistant, Betty, close the shop, and arrive home with a faint sensation of hope. Perhaps John will have run into so many problems that cancellation is the only way out. I misjudge him. Everything, as he says, is go! He has organised the building of a small platform at the side of the oval where bush makes a picturesque background, and he has borrowed some lighting from the next village. More! He has roped in May Cotter's donkey and Daphne's old milker, and a tethered nanny-goat with a kid.

'It doesn't say anything about goats.'

'It doesn't say there aren't any,' he retorts.

So there we all are, down at the oval. The sky is melon and apricot, and tiny clouds are dusted in like charcoal. Grazing kangaroos regard us with twitch-eared astonishment as we arrange ourselves on their dinner. The moon is almost ready to take centre stage, and the children are dressed in their middle-eastern blankets and tea-cloth head-dresses. Mary, a beautiful but slightly dim child, stares blankly ahead of her, waiting to 'go on'.

Quite a crowd is assembling. The fire had brought us together. Rugs and cushions litter the area before the stage. Music begins: John has his portable CD player. Suddenly I feel no sense of strain. I am not alone. We are a team.

A heavy truck grinds to a halt on the roadway. What now? 'What now, John?' I ask.

He grins. 'A secret.'

Out of the gloom comes a long neck with a fiercely proud head erect upon it. A camel! Two, three camels! John looks at me. 'Like it?'

I love it. I love everybody. I even love the Second Shepherd, who has just thrown up from all the excitement. Gabriel, nicely spot-lit, climbs onto a table carefully disguised with potted palms; and the old story begins.

'... *there went out a decree from Caesar Augustus* ... '

Knock-knock! The Innkeeper, Belle, comes forward.

'Have you room for us?' says diminutive Joseph. 'My wife's going to have a baby.'

Belle, the motel manager's daughter, stares at them with a professional eye. 'You're in luck,' she says. 'We've had a cancellation.'

Joseph stares back. 'You're not supposed to say that. You're supposed to say 'no room.''

Belle shrugs. She would have written it differently. 'OK then—no room.' She jerks her thumb. 'You can go round the back in the stable.'

By the time Joseph and Mary have done a round trip the cow has been manoeuvred into position and the donkey is standing with its rump to the audience. Somewhere a kookaburra begins to laugh, and I can understand how he feels. He is joined by a choral society of friends, and we are all, suddenly, a part of a much greater drama, a whole universe stretching above our heads, animals and birds and children and parents united in a vast and timeless exercise called love. I take John's hand in mine.

'Will you marry me?' he asks.

I nod. 'Yes, please—as soon as you like.'

Cicadas burst into a song of triumph. The First Shepherd, who has been given a lamb to carry, deposits it beside the crib and it gambols off into the dark bush. For a moment I think Joseph is going to pursue it. Three apprehensive little Wise Men lead their camels. 'I bring you frankinthenthe,' lisps the middle one. The four remaining members of the Heavenly Host do their best with Merv's arrangement, and all too soon it is over.

'Wonderful!' everyone is saying. 'Jane is *so* clever.'

'How will you beat *that* next year?' Mrs Vicar is asking.

I smile at John. Next year, if all goes to plan, I will have a proper excuse for not producing a nativity play. Any nativity happening this time next year will, I hope, be purely personal between John and me.

WINNING WAYS

This is an oddity. I had completely forgotten that I had written it, but it jumped out of my filing cabinet and said 'Use me! Use me!' I cannot even recall what gave me the idea or the format, but here it is, thrown to the critical wolves, and I hope somewhere there are folks who went through the same situation when their luck changed.

WINNING WAYS

Dad said, 'Spend it!' Mum said
'Don't you dare!'

Bernie said 'What about a motor bike?
A big one. A big one with them big wheels—
Yeah—why not?'

Mum said
'Don't talk silly, Bernie.'

Alice said 'Bali!
Always wanted to go to Bali—
Always wanted to! Crumbs—
It'd be fan*tas*tic, Mum.'

Mum said 'Look—
Let's keep a sense of proportion—
Why don't we?'

Gran said 'Runs through his fingers
Like water. Always did.
Just like his dad.'

The man at the deli said
'*Mama mia*! How much you say?
Mama mia—I never knew any rich people before.'

Dad said 'Save it, then.' Mum said
'There's things we need. It was my dollars.'

Pop said 'Knew a man once
Won money on a horse.'

Bernie said 'What happened?'

Pop sank another stubby. 'Bust his marriage.
Blew his brains out. Couldn't take it.'

Alice said 'Charming!
Musta been a nutter.'

Mum said 'There you are, then.
You gotta take these things easy.
You need stability. Or it'll all be gone—
And nothing to show.'

Dad said 'I suppose we can at least celebrate.
I suppose there's no harm in that?
Or is that not allowed either?'

Mum said 'You'll be grateful to me in the end.'

Gran said 'Always knows what's best for everyone!'

Mum said 'What did you say, Mother?'

Gran said nothing.

Dad said 'A new car!' Mum gave him one of her looks.
'A Rolls?' she said. 'Or a Mercedes?'

Bernie talked through a mouthful of chips.
No one understood him.

Alice painted her finger-nails. 'Like it?
It's "*My Passionate Heart*"—everyone's wearing it.'

Gran said 'Little trollop!' Bernie
Blew out a mouthful of chips on a laugh.

Mum
Wasn't pleased. But Pop nearly choked on his beer.

Dad said 'I reckon your mum's right.
It's a lotta money.
Could go to your head.' And he winked.

Alice looked at him, slowly. 'I reckon.
Mustn't get too excited. I might go out.'

Bernie said 'What about a . . . ?' and Dad
Glared at him. So Bernie said
'Oh, yeah, I get it.' And ate more chips.

Gran said 'When are we going to have tea?'

Pop opened another stubby. 'You'll drink yourself
Into an early grave,' said Gran.

'I'm eighty-five,' Pop said. 'No sweat!'

Mum looked at Dad. He was busy.
Alice was painting her toe-nails. Bernie
Was eating chips. Gran was inspecting her teeth.
Pop was scratching the top of his bald head.
Nobody said anything.

'All right! All right!' Mum said.
'Motor bikes and Bali and cars and all the rest!
But don't come complaining to me when it's all gone.'

163

Dad grinned. 'There'll be some change,' he said
'Out of a million dollars.'

Mum said 'I can't hardly believe it.
Can you?'

And Dad said 'We gotta celebrate! It won't seem real
Until we celebrate.'

And Mum smiled, a bit tearful,
And said 'You're probably right.'

And *I* said 'Hungry Jack's! Can we go to
Hungry Jack's? And buy the biggest whopper in the world?'

And Mum said 'Over my dead body! It's the Hilton—
Or nothing!'

I REMEMBER MISS PADDOCK

A bit of nostalgia now for those who remember the war years with all the stresses and strains of that time. Sadly, we don't seem to be able to avoid the friction that leads, inevitably it seems, to further conflicts; perhaps one day we will come to our senses and realise that there are other ways of living—if we could only find them. Meanwhile, some people will be affected more deeply than others, and so the pain continues.

This story grew out of a much-publicised episode which, at the time, made mothers all too conscious of what can happen when the stress becomes too great to bear.

I REMEMBER MISS PADDOCK

I remember Miss Paddock so well. 'Fish-face', we called her, with the natural progression of schoolgirl humour from Paddock to Haddock. Yet she was—though it would never have occurred to me then—an attractive woman, neat, orderly, coolly cheerful.

I see her now across the years as if I had met her yesterday, recalled for me by my mother's letter. She stood for ever in my mind before the class, her beige skirt smooth across neat hips, a narrow belt holding her immaculate shirt in place as mine never did. She was never hot, never wind-blown or sticky. There was about her a kind of dignity, withdrawn and untouchable.

'*I'm sure you'll be sorry to hear,*' my mother had written across seas and time, '*that Miss Paddock died recently. Mrs Prescott, I suppose I ought to say, but I never could think of her as married.*'

That was true enough. She had an aura of virginity about her that hardly went with the down-to-earthiness of marriage.

As a small girl, eight or nine, perhaps, I had adored Miss Paddock in a strange, impersonal way, possibly because she stood for all the things that I was not. I was tubby and untidy. My hair, when my mother occasionally decided to curl it, wound itself Medusa-like around my face, the carelessly twisted ends sticking out like paint brushes. I longed for the graceful sweep of gleaming golden hair that fell to her chin and neatly under, framing her small features. In a time when most women wore their hair rigidly waved, Miss Paddock's had a natural, controlled beauty that was typical of everything about her.

While I adored, I also despaired of ever becoming like her—and in fact never have!

'What a strange affair that was—about Miss P, I mean,' my mother's letter rambled on. *'Fancy after all those years! Dying like that, no family, they say. A very dark horse! You were very taken with her, I remember . . . '*

I could recall one occasion, even after so long, when my mother had lost patience. Childlike, I had imagined that my thoughts were unreadable.

'You and your Miss Paddock, Miss Paddock! You'd think she was God. You'll listen to me, young woman.'

And indeed, for that long, difficult year before the war, when the grown-ups so often seemed abstracted, she was my guiding light. And no doubt my mother was ever so slightly jealous of another woman's influence.

'Jealous of her!' she had exclaimed once, when I had teased her years afterwards. 'Jealous?' She had stared towards me thoughtfully, then shaken her head slowly. 'No, my dear, I was never jealous. But she was a strange woman, no doubt about it—we all felt it.'

'All?' I asked.

'All the mothers,' she said quietly. 'We used to talk about her while we were waiting for you to come out of school. She was deep . . . '

'You were jealous,' I laughed. 'Why deny it?'

The road to school was long and straight, leading through the village to the field where, steep-roofed and Victorian, the school stood. Sometimes, I remember, I would be passing the bus stop when Miss Paddock stepped from the bus, and we would walk together, chatting comfortably, along the half-mile of the main street. I cannot recall what we spoke about, only the feeling inside me as I was encouraged to give opinions on all kinds of things that normally I was expected to keep silence about. Grown-ups are not always perceptive, and my own parents were no better and no worse than any others; I never had to fear ridicule from Miss Paddock, and that, to a child, is not easily forgotten.

I can hardly claim that my thoughts ran on the late Mrs Prescott during the week after I received my mother's letter—it all seemed far away in space, if not in time. But from day to day I found she occupied my mind for a few moments here and there, and gradually I began to piece together little items, small recollections, tiny snatches of conversations long since dead; before my mind's eye Miss Paddock was taking shape and form.

Yet, what did I really know about her? She was all impression and no substance. She exuded an atmosphere of calm control, but there was nothing tangible about her. Her hand, when she had occasionally taken mine to guide it, was so cool, almost dry, that it hardly seemed flesh—fancy remembering that over so many years!

Where did she live? Once, boldly, I asked her.

'In a room,' she answered, 'high up in an old house. From the windows I can almost see the sea.'

It sounded no more substantial than the rest of her. Now, thousands of miles away, I tried to think where it could have been, this high, dream-like room. If she was anywhere near the sea she must have had a trying, tiring journey before she even started to teach us. And, too, she was obviously living in lodgings, so we still did not know where her roots were.

Then came the war. It was exciting for a nine year old. My father went off to death or glory, and I never realised the torment my mother must be feeling. Letters came from him, from dreary camps and then from depressing French billets, and still I was excited by the coming and going of troops through the village, the infrequent sight of a hostile plane flying high.

When the news came that my father was dead it seemed cruel that no one had warned me that we were not all playing a game. For a while the sun shone less brightly, and Miss Paddock was my support and comfort.

'War is bad and stupid,' she said to me—I can remember standing by her desk when the other children had gone out to play, so perhaps she had taken pity on my white-faced misery—'like a

169

little boy throwing stones in the playground because he is angry. But there are many good things that come out of war.'

I didn't understand, of course. But something about her face, her voice, comes back to me now. She had an omniscient way of saying the simplest things, so that one could not doubt her, and I felt a little cheered.

It must have been soon after that that I remember hearing my mother talking about Miss Paddock to the other mothers who stood stolidly at the school gate waiting for the bell to ring. Small gossip was a welcome relief to these women, so many bereaved, and Miss Paddock, as a 'foreigner' to the village, was fair game.

'What's courting?' I asked my best friend one day.

'Oh, *you* know,' she said, going limp; so I assumed it had something to do with love and soppy things like that. I didn't like to think of Miss Paddock—*my* Miss Paddock, if I was honest—having anything to do with men or marriage. For a few days I was distant with her, though I doubt if she noticed.

Then, one afternoon as we came hurtling out of school, there was a car waiting at the gate. Cars, by then, were a rarity; I think only the doctor and one or two others ran them in our tiny community. We children gathered round and stared without expression at the man sitting in the driver's seat. He stared back, possibly a little nervous at the eyes fixed on him, and then gave a wave of the fingers. At the direct approach we melted slowly away, backing towards our mothers.

'An officer!' I heard one say. 'From the camp, I expect. Fancy!'

'What does he want?' my mother asked, and then we saw Miss Paddock come slowly across the playground, hesitating when she saw the group at the gate. The man, smart in his uniform, leapt out of the car and opened the passenger door for her. We watched, country bumpkins all, as the car drew slowly away. She gave a small, regal gesture of her hand as she passed me, but I was too hurt to wave back.

'Well, well!' my mother said, and there were knowing glances and nodded heads as the car disappeared in the dust of the road.

I think that episode, simple and harmless as it was, marked the end of my infatuation for Miss Paddock. I spent more time in the playground and less standing by the door in case she should come out. I grew noisy and tomboyish, careless and cheerful, and her small rebukes no longer hurt me. But I lost the comfort of those gentle conversations, and regretted, in spite of my youth, the clay feet of my idol.

'Perhaps he's her brother?' someone said as the car, now a regular visitor, pulled away down the street. My mother smiled a superior smile and shook her head slowly.

'Looking at her like that? Nonsense!'

Whatever it was, it was no whirlwind romance—at least, not by wartime standards. For six months the car arrived two or three times a week and bore her away, before Miss Paddock sported a diamond on her left hand. There seemed little difference in her; she did not, as my more romantic friends hoped, glow with passion or desire. She remained cool as a churchyard lily, unflustered, serene.

'I wonder when the happy day will be?' someone asked as we moved away from the school gate.

'And whether we shall all be invited,' my mother said with a laugh. '*You'd* like to see Miss Paddock married, wouldn't you?' she said to me, and I muttered sulkily.

'Mutton dressed up,' one mother said darkly, with me not understanding a word.

'Well,' my mother conceded, 'she's no chicken. But she's still young enough.'

I had never thought of her as having any age. She seemed to me beyond such human failings as growing old. I watched her carefully, detecting with gloomy pleasure the faint lines from the corners of her eyes, the slight sagging of her chin. (Now, myself almost forty, I realise that she must have been the same age in those early days of war).

After the Easter holiday, taking everybody by surprise, she announced to us calmly that she was now Mrs Prescott, and we were to call her by her new name.

'Why?' asked some befuddled infant, and she smiled briefly and said that she had married Captain Prescott, and we could tell our mothers if we liked. They took two rooms in the village, and when he was able her husband came and lived there with her, though most of the time—and I was glumly glad of this—he was away in the camp, or going up to London, perhaps to conferences. He was friendly enough in a dry, abstract way that involved him in little contact. His wife, even when carrying a shopping basket and wielding ration books, still managed to remain ethereally perfect.

'She wouldn't suit my old man,' said my mother's friend. '*He* likes a bit of comfort!' I didn't know what she meant, but I half understood the wink and the nudge. Mother shrugged.

'*He* wouldn't suit me,' she said, and I remembered the jollity of my father, the warmth and laughter he had generated before the French fields had claimed him. 'If you ask me, they're well suited to each other.'

I have no idea how long the marriage followed its placid way before Captain Prescott was called away to a new area of the war. School was closed one day while Mrs Prescott went to see him off in London; then, for a while, life returned to what it had been before his arrival on the scene. I was glad. I liked my grown-ups predictable, and now that I was older I didn't much like what I knew of marriage.

'How's your Mrs Prescott?' my mother asked from time to time, ignoring the fact that she was no longer mine. 'She's a wonder. How she goes on teaching all you young monkeys, knowing where he is, beats me.'

'Where is he, then?'

'In the desert.' She sounded surprised. 'Doesn't she talk about him?'

'What desert?'

'North Africa. Fancy, doesn't she tell you anything about him? You'd think she'd use it for geography, wouldn't you?'

Miss Paddock, we sometimes called her now, reverting subconsciously. Sometimes she stopped us, and sometimes she

172

didn't. Sometimes, I now think, she found it difficult to believe that she really had been married for those brief months.

I suppose the women were half expecting the news that came one morning. The village grapevine had the contents of the telegram broadcast almost before she had time to absorb the words that told her that Captain Prescott had died the owner of a high decoration for courage.

Probably every child in the school was warned about behaviour. My mother wept for her as she had not wept since my father's death; and I, susceptible to atmosphere, wept too, enjoying the abandonment to anguish. School was closed for a week, and then we returned, round-eyed and apprehensive, to cope with something that we still didn't quite understand. But we needn't have worried. Mrs Prescott was in command of herself, at least before the children, and life rolled on reassuringly.

I wonder when it was, not much later, surely, that we arrived at school one Monday morning to find a new teacher installed. We were taken by surprise, and so were our parents. A note was sent home with each one of us, and I remember watching my mother reading hers and clucking anxiously like an old hen.

'What *is* it?' I asked urgently. 'What's happened?'

'Your Mrs Prescott,' she said, reading it again. 'She's collapsed and the doctor's sent her away for a rest. You're to have this new teacher until she comes back—what's her name?'

'Miss Briggs,' I said, imagining Mrs Prescott collapsing in a heap on the floor, dramatically crushed under the burden of her husband's death. 'What *is* collapsed?'

'Tired out, I expect. No wonder, with all of you hanging around her all the time.'

'You didn't collapse. When Dad died, you didn't get tired and collapse.'

She put her hand under my chin and smiled at me, and I remember noticing for the first time how weary her eyes were, how her mouth folded down at the corners until she smiled.

'I had you,' she said quietly. 'She has no one.'

Miss Briggs was fun, stout and exuberant and efficient. We learned things we had never known before, we played games with energetic abandon; treacherously, I began to hope that Mrs Prescott would stay collapsed. There were no emotions with Miss Briggs, just hearty good fun and hard work. So when, one day, I saw my former teacher walking along the street, I turned and slipped round the corner, going home another way.

All the way I pondered on what I had seen, and when I sat in the kitchen watching my mother baking I asked her if she had heard anything about—well, anything!

'Anything about anything? What on earth do you mean, child?' She turned and looked at me, amused.

'Oh, nothing.' But suddenly the news burst out of me. 'I've seen Mrs Prescott. And she was pushing a pram!'

I was well satisfied by the reception of my offering. Mother turned and stared, floury hands still.

'A pram? Are you sure it was Mrs Prescott?'

'Of course I am. Can I have a bun?'

'No, wait.' She turned the dough without looking at it. 'Are you *quite* sure? Well, of course you are. But a baby . . . !'

'I thought she collapsed.' I put my finger into the rationed jam.

'Don't do that,' she said automatically. 'Yes—so did I.'

The news took the female population of the village by storm. Opinion varied between thinking how nice it was that now she would have something to remember the Captain by, to speculations as to what sort of mother she would make. I can remember that the baby, when I occasionally saw him, was beautifully turned out, and that Mrs Prescott spent a great deal of time knitting.

But the women shook their heads together anxiously as time went on.

'It's not natural,' they said. 'Keeping so much to herself. It'll be bad for both of them.' And even the children noticed how detached she was, how difficult it was to talk to her, how jealously she guarded the child. We, who had romped and rolled together since birth, would have liked nothing better than to have been allowed to play with the baby; but somehow, without a word spoken, we knew that we must never ask.

I wrote back to my mother.

'I was sorry to hear of Miss Paddock/Prescott. It has brought back many memories. She was rather a strange creature, wasn't she? How odd to think she must have been quite an elderly woman when she died. For me, she has always been ageless.'

And there she would have sat, for ever knitting in her little front garden, at least in my memory. But something was tugging at my mind, trying to get into the open. Now and again I frowned, puzzled, trying to recall anything at all connected with Mrs Prescott and her baby. But it was a blank. I lived in the village for another ten years until I was swept off to the States by an impulsive bridegroom; but I have no recollection of seeing the baby grow up, or of watching Mrs Prescott going about the village shops. All I could remember was a stirring of something faintly unpleasant, something better forgotten.

But my adult mind would not wilfully forget as our childish ones had done. I worried at the problem and got nowhere. At last I wrote again, going out and posting the letter at once, as if by doing so I could expect a quicker answer from my mother. It seemed an age before the blue envelope dropped into my mailbox.

'You have got stirred up about Mrs P, haven't you?' (You and your Mrs Prescott, I seemed to hear again!) *'It was rather sad, I'm afraid. We were more reticent then, and we thought, rightly or wrongly, that children should be protected from such things. These days children seem to know everything from the cradle. When we were children . . . '* ('Oh, get on, get on!' I muttered, skipping chunks of spidery writing).

' . . . there was something wrong, we all knew it, although we tried to imagine that we were mistaken. There was a look in her eyes, not fear, a sort of wildness that kept you at a distance . . . (so I had been right about that, anyway) *. . . she made no friends, just looked after the baby, nothing else, all the time. And then there were the dates, you see. Nothing you could prove, but it just seemed wrong, I mean for the baby to be so big, and she didn't look pregnant, somehow,*

when she left—nothing you could prove, as I said, but you can't fool a bunch of country women.

'Anyway, it was all hushed up, but the police came one day, plain clothes so that no one was sure, but you can't hide those feet, and she went away, sitting in the corner of the car like a little animal, all that lovely hair tangled, clutching the baby to her. (Was everyone out on the street watching? I wondered cynically).

' *... the case came to court just as something rather tremendous happened in the war, I can't remember what, not Normandy, that was later ...* (What case? What case? I cried, shuffling through the flimsy sheets for an answer). *'She went to pieces when they took the baby away and put her in a home, you know, a mental place. She stayed there, so I heard, for years, then went into a private one, and was there till she died. Tragic, all those wasted years. I suppose really it was because she married late, and then losing him like that before they had settled down properly ... though I always thought there was something funny about her, that awful self-control, it made you wonder what she was controlling.'*

I went through the letter again, but I could find no trace of what I was looking for. What had happened? Why had they taken the baby away? What was all that about dates? I sat down and wrote.

' *... you forgot the most important thing. What was the court case about?'*

In due, unhurried course my mother's letter came.

'I thought I told you. Perhaps you didn't read it properly! Mrs Prescott was accused of abducting someone else's baby. She kept it for nearly four months before they caught her. She stole it out of a pram in the north of England. By the time the parents had got it back they had given it up for dead. It was a wicked thing to do ...'

I sat for a long time with the letter in my hands. I saw the cool, immaculate Miss Paddock; I saw the Captain, tall, not bad-looking; I saw the baby, holding up his hands in the pram and apparently quite happy and contented. And I could sense across the years, for the first time, the depths of passion and longing in the neat, orderly breast of Mrs Prescott. Depths which, at last, had swept up and overwhelmed her.

My mother had got it right, as usual. *'It made you wonder what she was controlling.'*

THE GARDENER

When I was a child we had a gardener called Fellowes. That's the only reason I can think of for writing this story, though anyone who has employed a gardener with attitude may well appreciate the subtleties involved in persuading him to carry out instructions. Gardeners always know best! Female gardeners, of course, are a different proposition, warm, friendly, lovers of tiny plants and nurturers of the ones that want to die. They are nothing like Bert Fellowes in this story.

THE GARDENER

Twittering Parva is known for its cottage gardens, each neatly kept—each at some time in its history the responsibility of Bert Fellowes. He is an old man now, past eighty, but there is a certain cachet in securing his services in the garden.

'The begonias are a picture, aren't they? But, of course, Bert Fellowes comes once a week.'

Social status attaches to the time of day that Bert allocates to you and your garden. In the mornings, of course, he is full of beans, and the work goes with a swing. In the afternoons the pace is a little more leisurely, a little less inspired. There are some unlucky folk who cannot entice him into their herbaceous borders until the evening, and then life can only be sustained with constant supplies of beer and the odd fag. But it's still worth employing him.

Jennie and Donald Thomson came to the village when the gardens were lying dormant, between snow and spring. It was not long before they began to regard the growth of nature with alarm, much as Jack must have stared aghast at the beanstalk.

'We shall have to do something,' Jennie said.

'But what?' asked Donald.

'Of course,' said their neighbour kindly, 'you need Bert Fellowes. A genius! Five green fingers on each hand.'

'We'll get him,' the young Thomsons said, relieved.

The neighbour smiled a superior smile. 'Man disposes,' she said. 'But Bert decides for himself.'

179

Jennie Thomson met him by the village green one lunch time. Sarah Jane was fretful in her pram, lunch was due, but Mr Fellowes must be approached sooner or later.

'I wonder,' said Jennie cautiously, 'if you have time spare for gardening?'

Bert stared into the distance, his knobbly fingers busy in a tin of tobacco from which he suddenly produced a limp, hand-rolled cigarette. Jennie wondered if he had heard her.

'My husband gets in rather late,' she said apologetically. Bert lit his mangled fag and blew out a cloud of evil-smelling smoke.

'And I'm not allowed to do any heavy work . . . '

Really, she thought, he would make a marvellous detective. All that silence made one want to babble.

'So we thought . . . '

'Marnin' or arternoon?'

Jennie jumped. 'Well, that's up to you really. When could you come?'

Bert seemed disappointed that she had not fallen into his trap. 'Well, I hain't got a marnin' right now,' he said slowly. 'An' I hain't rightly got an arternoon.' He spat over his shoulder and Jennie looked away. 'I might fit you in on Friday evenin'.'

Jennie nodded quickly. 'That will be lovely. I'll tell my husband.' Sarah Jane grizzled in the pram. 'See you on Friday.'

Bert kept his eyes on the middle distance.

On Friday the garden was cleared of all Sarah Jane's toys, and Jennie hovered nervously by the kitchen window until the bent form of Mr Fellowes appeared at the gate.

'It's not the grass,' she said as she led him round to the back. 'We have an ancient mower to do that. It's the borders,' and she waved her arm at the untidy flower beds. 'There are some very nice plants under all that.' She laughed nervously.

Bert moved ponderously forward. 'Hasn't changed much. I remember putting in them shrubs for Mrs Williamson—that'd be back in . . . ' he scratched his head, 'back in the fifties.'

Jennie stared at him. 'Gracious!' she said.

'An' that weepin' willer—that went in for her old dad, round about end of the war. The second war,' he explained, and Jennie nodded as if it mattered.

'We've let it go a little, I'm afraid. But we've only been here six months.'

Bert gazed around him. 'Won't take long,' he conceded. 'Now, I've seen gardens . . . ' he began to take off his jacket, and Jennie rushed to help him, ' . . . what have been so neglected . . . ' He made his way to the shed and stopped short. 'What's this?'

Jennie swallowed. 'It's the motor mower.' His face registered nothing but disgust. 'I know it's not very beautiful—but it's rather old, and it does the job pretty well, and my husband's very fond of it.' For a moment it seemed that Bert's employment hung in the balance; then he grunted and moved on to the fork and spade.

'I've heard them talking about it,' he growled. 'Right infernal machine, it looks.'

For a blissful few weeks Bert made his way to the gate on a Friday evening, and gradually the garden returned to its former beauty. Jennie, glancing out of the window, would see the old man moving with the deceptively slow walk of the true gardener, and as he moved, the plants stood up straighter and the flowers bloomed more vigorously. But he still regarded the mower with distaste, and if Jennie was not in sight he would spit into the earth beside its ugly, oil-spattered body. Infernal machine!

'Used to cut the lawn for Mrs Williamson's dad,' he said reminiscently, scowling at the garden fork. 'Nice little machine he had, an' a roller. Can't beat a nice roller. There wasn't a daisy on that lawn for her old dad.' He decided against spitting and rolled himself a cigarette. Jennie stared sadly at the daisies, which she secretly loved, seeing herself in a few months' time making daisy chains for Sarah Jane to wear. But she had been told that the daisies had to go.

'Seven years,' he said, from behind his smoke-screen. 'That's how long I was getting this garden into shape. After that I worked at Colonel Smythe's.' He grew silent, recalling the old days, then he pulled himself up as straight as his old bones would allow. 'Thirty-nine to forty-five I grew taties.'

He went back to his weeding.

That weekend Donald broke a bone in his wrist, and the great bucking bronco of a mower was beyond his control.

'You'll have to ask the old boy,' he said unsympathetically.

'He'll never do it,' she cried, panicking.

'You could ask.'

Bert Fellowes stared at her when she made her request. His expression was one of such outrage that she shut the door and leaned on it, waiting for him to give in his notice. But in a few minutes she saw him at work on the sweet peas and heaved a sigh of relief.

Suddenly the calm of the summer evening was broken by a great roar, and Jennie raced to the window. Bert Fellowes, legs braced, false teeth set, stood with the monster at one end of the garden while it belched smoke and oil over everything within sight. As he put it into gear Jennie sat down and put her hands over her ears.

But there was no crash. Bert made a perfect landing by the back door, waved to her gleefully, and charged on. The monster roared and growled, consuming its weekly allowance of grass, and Bert leapt, goblin-like, behind it.

At the end of the allotted time, Bert came to the back door, wiping his face with an oily cloth. Jennie paid him, silent and astonished.

'I been thinkin',' he said casually. 'I could give you a marnin', if you like.' Jennie nodded speechlessly.

It was the beginning of the end. Jennie and Donald have the best-mown lawn in Twittering Parva . . . but oh! the herbaceous borders! He simply won't look at them.

PRIDE IN PERSEPHONE

And so we come back to Persephone Downs. Myrtle and her little family are thriving, and the seasons come and go with their usual dramas and set-backs. But even in this peaceful backwater it is impossible to ignore what is going on in the great big world outside. There is a stirring of national consciousness from Sydney to Melbourne; Perth and Adelaide and Brisbane are making plans for the biggest ever party; television crews, caterers of every size and clientele, and makers of things that go bang in the night, are all sweating over their contribution to the celebrations. Wives of mayors are polishing the mayoral chains for their husbands. Schools are trying to teach the words of the National Anthem to their students.

You can bet, with Myrtle stirring the pot, that Persephone Downs will not be left out.

It's the Bicentennial!

PRIDE IN PERSEPHONE

When the first faint trumpet fanfares of the Bicentennial rejoicings came to Persephone Downs (pop: 576), no one took any notice.

It sounded—as Mr Padstow said, lugubriously surveying a week-old newspaper—like 'another bloody bash, more bloody money down the drain!'

'Language!' said Mrs Padstow automatically, and her daughter Myrtle, who had called in with the three infant Thirkells, put her hands over the eldest child's ears.

'What's wrong with spending a bit of money?' Myrtle said. 'Better than buying all those bombs and things.'

'That's not the point,' her father said, sipping tea noisily. 'Who needs a celebration? What's it for? Why can't they leave us alone?'

Mrs Padstow said, with a thoughtful look in her eye that a bit of jollification wouldn't come amiss in Persephone Downs, and her husband snorted.

'Always after the bright lights! That's the trouble with folks today.'

'Bright lights?' Mrs Padstow quelled him with a look. 'Me? Half yer luck!'

He shifted the paper defensively and cast a glance at his daughter, busy suckling her youngest with a distant expression in her eyes. Unobservant he often was, indeed, but anyone who knew Myrtle understood—and sometimes feared—that abstracted air: she had had an idea.

185

'We've had plenty of excitement,' he said, glaring at his helpmeet over his glasses. 'What about the satellite? Persephone's never been hit by a satellite before. Isn't that enough for you?'

'That was last year,' Mrs Padstow said, slamming the lid on a cast-iron pot of soup on the wood boiler. 'Besides, everybody'll be celebrating. Why shouldn't we?'

Myrtle grinned at her mother as she detached the baby's parasitic little mouth from its supply. 'We'll make the place sit up, eh, Mum? What'll it be? A party?'

'For a whole year?' Her father gazed at her in alarm.

'Well—perhaps only six months!' She laughed at the horror on his face. 'You might even enjoy it, Dad.'

She gathered her brood and left in her usual whirlwind of energy; at the car she looked at her mother quizzically.

'I didn't think *you'd* be interested, Mum. Not your style.'

Mrs Padstow surveyed the rolling hectares, the distant cattle, the stubbled ground on which her husband's sweat had helped a record crop to grow; at the blue of the sky, and the sudden flash of green as a brace of parrots swept across the track; at the old barn leaning drunkenly to one side, the stripped-down tractor within it, the fences that needed repairing and the dam that was two-thirds empty; and suddenly she sighed.

'Well, I was young meself once. I can remember what it felt like. Persephone needs a bomb under it once in a while.' She gave a dry, unhumorous laugh. 'Bicentennial? Two hundred years of what? Sweat and labour and heartache and suffering! That's what.'

Myrtle laughed gently. 'Go on with you, Mum. It's not all bad.' She nodded towards the Thirkell babies, scrapping in the car. '*They've* got a future, haven't they, little perishers? We've done a lot wrong—but we got some of it right.'

'Well—set your bomb and light your fuse. I can see you've got an idea. Nothing'll stop you, will it?'

'Nope—nothing!' Myrtle kissed her mother, swept herself into the car and was off, one hand waving out of the window, the other changing gears and chastising children, towards the distant

186

farm gate that led to Persephone. Mrs Padstow wiped her hands on her apron and watched her out of sight; then turned towards the homestead and Mr Padstow.

'Is she going to do something I'll regret?' he asked as she closed the door behind her. Mrs Padstow regarded him thoughtfully.

'I hope so,' she retorted, and filled the kettle noisily.

Myrtle sat up in bed, deep in thought. Brian, up all the previous night with a sick cow, slipped in and out of sleep, disturbed by the lamp above his head.

'Are you going to sit up all night,' he asked tetchily.

'Hm-hmm!' Myrtle said absently, sliding down and putting the light out in one movement.

'What's the matter with you? Can't you sleep?'

'I was thinking about the best way to get people together to have a bit of fun.'

'So was I!' said her husband, and proceeded to show her one method.

'That wasn't quite what I meant,' she said eventually. 'But it's certainly effective!'

The notice on the board at the general stores said:

WHAT DOES PERSEPHONE DOWNS WANT TO
DO TO CELEBRATE
AUSTRALIA'S BICENTENARY?
WHAT DO **YOU** *WANT TO DO?*

Such directness could only have come from one who, like Myrtle née Padstow, avoided deviousness like the devil. 'If you want a straight answer,' she sometimes said to Brian, who didn't have her gift, 'you must ask a straight question.'

Of the answers 'posted' in the box under the notice board, three were very rude, two abhorred innovations in any form, and four made positive suggestions. Myrtle spread these out on the kitchen table after the children had gone to bed, and before Brian returned from his nightly jar at the Swagman's Arms.

'*Have a party,*' said the first with disarming simplicity.

'Why not?' said Myrtle.

'*Do up the village hall,*' the second suggested. The third favoured a weekend festival, with cricket, side-shows, kids' sports, and a home-made variety show to wind up. Myrtle pulled a face. That was from Prunella Devine, for sure, looking for somewhere to air her repertoire. (Prunella had sung in G&S, and liked people to know it).

'*We ort to have a pop consert. Why cant we have a proper group like Moldering Corspses?*' Eddie Devine, that would be, he of the Elvis haircut. His mother's singing talents had emerged in him in a slightly warped variation.

'What if we have a festival?' Myrtle said as she and Brian drank cocoa together before bed.

'What for?'

'For the Bicentenary!' she said impatiently. 'To celebrate!' A festival, and a special cricket match, and a variety show, and splosh a bit of paint round the village hall, and raise some money and . . . '

'Hang on! How long's this bi-bi-cent-wot's-it?'

'A year.'

'We gotta keep going for a year? Can't be done. What about sowing—and harvesting and . . . '

'Not *all* the time, silly. But what do you think?'

Brian thought deeply, staring into the sweetened mud of his nightcap. 'It makes me feel very tired,' he said at last. Myrtle sighed. Must she always go it alone?

It would be time-consuming to follow Myrtle through the next action-packed months. Enough to say that Prunella Devine was appointed to present a variety show (Persephone Junior Singers were already rehearsing *The Road to the Isles* and *Click go the Shears*), preceded by an afternoon of sport and cricket (organised by Brian against his better judgement), and a great celebration lunch prior to that. The only idea that evaporated without trace was the pop concert, and even young Eddie never really expected anything else.

'Perhaps we could inject a little culture into it,' the Reverend Mr Tonks said diffidently. 'My brother-in-law is a very fine organist. I'm sure he would come.'

'What—sit in a cold church and listen to yonder squeeze-box?' said Myrtle's grandfather-in-law, Grandad Thirkell, whose Yorkshire accent intensified under pressure.

'Well, I wouldn't have . . . ' Mr Tonks said, slightly hurt. 'It's not a bad little instrument. And my brother-in-law . . . '

'Save 'is breath to cool 'is porridge!' Mr Thirkell said, lighting his pipe with explosive bursts of flame and a bonfire of smoke.

'Well, really! My dear Mr Thirkell . . . !'

Myrtle soothed him with smiles and mischievous glances towards her husband's unrepentant grandfather. 'He doesn't mean it,' she whispered. 'He likes to get his cats and pigeons properly stirred up.' Mr Tonks nodded, his face stiff; and no one else suggested that Persephone's celebrations should be sullied by the administration of a spoonful of culture.

'That sort o' thing,' Mr Thirkell said in a penetrating whisper, 'belongs in t'city, not out here. Organs! I'd tell 'em what to do with theer organs!'

It was hard work getting everything to fruition. Soothing ruffled feathers became a daily occupation for Myrtle, as pecking orders were established in areas not normally open to the inhabitants of Persephone Downs.

'What's the matter with everybody?' she demanded as Brian sat down to his tea. 'Why can't they get it all together without squabbling?' She banged his plate in front of him. 'There's Prunella sulking because Mrs Glenn from the bakery once sold a loaf to Joan Sutherland, and Mrs Ashleigh is ropeable because you didn't let her husband captain the cricket team. Why didn't you? She won't speak to me.'

He took a tentative poke at a half-cooked sausage with his fork. The cooking had fallen off badly. 'He's only got one leg,' he said mildly. 'What does she want—a hopping match!'

'I know he can't run. But he could have someone run for him.' He looked up at her, and she sat down suddenly and gave a shaky laugh. 'No, of course you're right. I'm sorry.'

Brian misread the signs. 'While you're being sorry, take pity on this . . . ' He rolled the pale object round the plate. He didn't see her threatening eyebrow. 'I like them crisp and sizzling, not pale and underdone.'

In grim silence Myrtle took the plate, removed the sausage between delicate fingers, and dropped it into the wood-burning stove. A flash of flame acknowledged the unexpected offering.

'In about two minutes,' she said with acid sweetness, 'it should be all you desire!' She wiped her fingers like Pilate washing his hands and stalked to the door. 'I'm going to bed!' she announced with lofty disdain. 'Don't waken me.'

Brian let out a long sigh. One thing was certain: his marriage would never reach its bicentenary at this rate. But that was women for you—no sense of humour, everything taken to heart, and emotional outbursts without warning or reason.

He opened the top of the stove. There, in a cocoon of flame, lay the sausage. He took a toasting fork from the wall and prodded until he impaled his prey and lifted it carefully out. With an air of satisfaction he placed it on his plate among the cooling vegetables. She'd been right about that, anyway. It was exactly as he liked a sausage to be—richly brown and curved like a boomerang.

So, in fits and starts like a poorly-maintained farm truck, Persephone's celebrations took shape. The Day, as had been arranged, was sunny and cloudless, and people turned out in force, some in period dress. The slow bicycle race was full of drama and broken knees, and the cricket match was notable for the highest score ever seen in the shire. Brian was ecstatic.

Gingerly the men lit the old stove in the hall for the evening's supply of tea and coffee, and the smoke had cleared nicely by the time Prunella sang 'O my beloved father'. Grandad Thirkell astonished no one by conjuring tricks in which a coin clearly changed hands to amaze only the three-year-olds, and dropped the egg he had apparently just swallowed to amaze only the youngest. But he raised a better laugh than Nobby Gribbett, the butcher, who told several dreadful stories and forgot the punch-line in each. Myrtle's face burned with embarrassment for him.

At last it was all over: except for the real excitement of the day (though more accurately it was early the following morning).

Myrtle, restless and over-stimulated, left her warm bed and stood by the window. Stars shone above. She opened the fly-screen and leaned out. Somewhere a bird squawked, and over the trees the sky . . .

She stared. It looked like sunset, but it was to the east and nowhere near dawn.

'It's the hall!' she cried. 'Brian, it's the hall!'

It was a splendid sight, if you like that kind of thing. The old wooden building went up and subsided into itself with a mighty show of sparks and a roar like a strong wind. There was little danger—no trees stood close and there was gravel all around. But its going would leave a gap in the community.

'Fancy!' said Myrtle, standing with Brian as the citizens of Persephone Downs made their way home in the early dawn and the firies rolled up their hoses. 'All that time, all that money, all those meetings and making things and planning and organising . . . '

Brian put his arm around her and squeezed her. 'And all thanks to you!'

She grinned suddenly, the weariness all at once gone. 'And there's not a thing to show for it, not a thing, except . . . ' She held her hands out to the dying embers. 'Except a pile of ashes and no hall! I think we've short-changed ourselves.'

'We'll build a new one—in brick.'

She looked up at him. 'What was it all for?'

Brian stared over her head thoughtfully to where the sun was rising. 'It was a matter of pride. Pride in being Australian, in being country folk, in belonging to Persephone Downs. Pride in Persephone!'

Myrtle drew her coat warmly around her. 'I'd forgotten for a moment. That's it, of course.'